COASTAL CRUISE

COASTAL ADVENTURES SERIES VOLUME 11

DON RICH

Library of Congress PCN Data

Rich, Don

Coastal Cruise/Don Rich

Florida Refugee Press LLC

Cover by: Cover2Book.com

This is a work of fiction. Names, characters, and incidents are either the product of the author's imagination or are used fictitiously. Any resemblance to actual persons, living or dead, businesses, companies, events, or locales is purely coincidental. However, the overall familiarity with boats and water found in this book comes from the author having spent years on, under, and beside them.

Published by FLORIDA REFUGEE PRESS LLC

Crozet, VA

To my friend Eric Cottell, a truly amazing person and an inspiring inventor. One of these days, I'll take you up on that offer to stay aboard Providence.

PROLOGUE

E *arly Saturday morning...*

"Meowww."

Sandy Morgan felt the small weight on his chest before he heard his alarm clock go off. Opening his eyes and looking through the porthole beside his bed, he saw there wasn't even a hint of light from the coming dawn yet. The red LED numbers on the clock on the table next to him showed it was only a few minutes before five.

"Mrrrowww!"

"Jeeze, KC, that was my ear, not a microphone!" Sandy turned and could just make out the outline of his feline boatmate by the low nightlight coming from the companionway behind him. Though it wasn't enough light for him to see the swat of the cat's paw that was about to impact his nose.

"Hey! What the hell is up with you this morning? It's way too early for your breakfast." Another swat. "Oh, alright. But don't make this a habit."

Sandy turned on the light next to the bed and sat up. That was when he saw the strange look on his cat's face. A look he'd never seen before—a mixture of both fear and alarm. Something he never expected to see on the face of a tough cat who had been born and survived his first days in the marsh on Ocracoke Island in the Outer Banks of North Carolina. There he'd lived a feral life until he was trapped and neutered by a local animal welfare group called Ocracats.

Two of Ocracats' best foster families then tried everything to domesticate KC, to no avail. With no other alternative, he was turned out on the island to live the rest of his life where he'd been born. But instead of returning to the marsh, he'd taken to hanging around a store that was owned by the head of Ocracats. Every day she fed a group of feral cats there that preferred village life over the marsh. That's when one-year-old KC—previously known as Larry—took up residence under the covered porch on the front of her store. That is until the day Sandy showed up. It was like Larry had been biding his time, waiting around for him to arrive. He followed Sandy back to his fifty-five-foot trawler named *Epilogue*, which the cat promptly boarded without waiting for an invitation. The boat became his adopted new home that came equipped with KC's very own human staff.

Sandy was a bestselling author, and at that point in his mid-sixties, he had already been a widower for two years. He lived and worked aboard *Epilogue* with his niece Micah Monroe. From Ocracoke, the trio then traveled down to Florida and eventually back to Virginia together—the cat having taken to their floating lifestyle almost instantly.

"Larry" was quickly renamed KC after Sandy's good friend Casey Shaw. He'd been the one who had first suggested that Sandy make Ocracoke a stop on his travels back and forth. KC had now become a fixture on his new roomie's writing desk on the back deck. Sandy even had a cat door installed in the aft cabin bulkhead so that KC could come and go as he pleased. This was a necessary accommodation since his human had drawn the line at keeping a litter box aboard. But the tall, dark gray-and-black tabby never seemed to venture far from his human companion and always found his way home each night.

Sandy slipped on shorts and a tee shirt, then made a quick stop at the head before going to the galley to open a can of cat food for KC. But when he put it in a dish and set it on the deck, KC ignored it completely.

"Mrrrowww!" The cat looked up at him expectantly, then took off for the steps leading up to the salon. Turning around, he glared at Sandy, then came back and swatted his leg, this time with claws extended.

"Owww! What the hell, KC?"

In response, KC ran over to the back bulkhead next to his cat door. "Mrrrroowwww!" This time it was in a more demanding tone that contained a sense of urgency.

Sandy watched as KC shot through the cat door. When Sandy didn't immediately follow him outside, he came back in and did a complete circle to get his human's attention before racing back out.

In frustration, Sandy said, "Crazy-assed cat," even though there was no other human aboard to hear it since Micah had long since moved off the boat to live with her boyfriend.

Opening the door to the aft deck, he spotted KC waiting by the gangway. The look on the cat's face seemed to say, *Now you're getting it —come on!* KC ran down the gangway onto the floating dock and over to an access ramp that led up to land. By the dim light coming from the dock lights, Sandy could see the cat turn around again with that expectant look.

This was totally out of character for what could normally be described as an "extremely chill" cat. But Sandy was fond of telling friends about how "cats know things"—something that KC had proven on more than one occasion. He'd displayed an almost eerie sixth sense about certain upcoming events. But this current behavior was still way out of character for Sandy's feline pal.

"Okay, KC, I get it; you want me to follow you. Lead on." Sandy was curious about what might be behind this unusual pre-dawn wake-up call.

KC raced across the parking area and over to the path that led through a group of tall and bushy evergreens. These hid the security fence which separated the adjacent *Mallard Cove Marina* from *Casey's Cove*. This latter cove was part of a secluded twenty-one-acre property owned by his friends, Casey and Dawn Shaw. Its main feature was a small, deep-water, natural basin that was home to their 110-foot Hargrave yacht, *Lady Dawn*, the couple's floating home.

After Casey and Dawn bought this property, they added several additional slips. These now contained the boats and houseboats of a handful of their closest live-aboard friends, including Sandy.

Sandy followed the dimly lit pathway through the trees and over to a gate in the fence, where he saw KC impatiently waiting for him. The cat squeezed through the narrow space between the fence and the gate and then waited on the other side as Sandy opened it. Once he was through, KC took off again, disappearing around the corner of *Mallard Cove Marina's* large dry-stack boat barn.

Making his way across the pavement surrounding the large metal building, Sandy was now able to move faster in the bright wash of its security lights. He had to slow again when the spill from those lights ran out when he reached the walkway alongside the marina basin's bulkhead. Like the path between the trees, this walkway was also dimly lit. But there was still enough light to see KC far ahead. He was running toward the *Cove Restaurant's* deck, a couple of hundred yards in the distance. But at the corner of the basin where charter boat row began, the cat stopped short and again looked back. Now his look had changed to a combination of impatience as well as urgency.

As Sandy got close to him, he said in a hushed voice, "What the hell, KC? I can't even get breakfast at the *Cove* yet; they don't open for another half hour."

But instead of continuing to the restaurant's deck, the cat turned and ran down the ramp to the floating dock that ran parallel to the restaurant and along behind the charter boats. As Sandy reached the ramp, he saw KC turn out onto the finger pier between the two boats that comprise Captain Bill "Baloney" Cooper's Dolphin Fleet. The nearest boat was Baloney's original *Golden Dolphin*, an older forty-eight-foot custom New Jersey sport fisherman that had been Bill and his wife Betty's home for many years. But now KC leaped into the fishing cockpit of the second boat, an older and much larger rebuilt Viking convertible sportfish called *My Mahi*. It had become their new home two years ago.

As far as Sandy knew, this area wasn't part of KC's normal territory. Instead, he usually preferred to shun all the tourists and people by staying on the grounds of *Casey's Cove*. Though it hit Sandy suddenly as he realized that KC *had* squeezed through the security gate like he'd done it before. And now he'd disappeared into *My Mahi*'s dark fishing cockpit.

There were flood lamps focused on all the boats in charter boat row from poles up on the *Cove*'s deck, but they were dark now and would only come on when the restaurant opened. A couple of boats farther down the row had their own cockpit flood lamps that stayed on all night, but no one lived aboard those like on *My Mahi*. Bill and Betty preferred having their privacy at night and only turned on their cockpit lights when they were expecting guests.

Again, in a low voice, Sandy hissed, "C'mon, KC, get out of there! We need to go home."

In response, a low moan came from the cockpit, and it definitely wasn't from the cat. Alarmed, Sandy hurried out onto that same finger pier, staring into the dark cockpit. He could just make out KC standing next to a figure who was lying prone on the deck. Sandy jumped over the gunwale, hurrying over to the figure, which turned out to be Bill Cooper. He was dressed in pajamas, and the shirt portion was soaked in blood. A knife handle protruded from the upper right portion of his chest. He was gasping for breath.

"Oh my God, Bill! Stay still; I'll get help."

Struggling to get the words out, Cooper almost whispered, "No... help Betty; she's hurt bad." He slowly raised a hand, pointing at the cabin door before that arm fell back to the deck.

Torn between wanting to help Bill and needing to check on Betty, Sandy reluctantly left him and went into the cabin to see about his other friend. He quickly returned, switching on the cockpit floodlights on his way back out. In the bright light, the scene was far worse than it originally appeared in the dark. Bill had apparently fought his assailant in the salon, then down the cockpit steps. There was a trail of blood leading to where he fell, and it was pooling around him, coming from several wounds in his torso and arms. Sandy reached into his pocket for his cell phone before realizing he'd left it back on *Epilogue*.

Bill's eyes were now closed as he'd lost consciousness. Sandy knew he'd need to put pressure on the worst of the wounds to try and staunch the bleeding. He also knew he needed to get medics here pronto, or he'd be wasting his time trying to stop the bleeding by himself. Without their help, Sandy would only be prolonging the inevitable; the key was to get the medics on the way fast. He also knew not to remove the knife himself since that could cause even more damage. That was a job for a surgeon at the hospital, and he had to get Bill there ASAP. Out of the corner of his eye, he saw the restaurant lights coming on inside. He made the tough decision to leave Bill in order to get more help. Sandy raced up onto the restaurant's deck and began pounding on the glass door.

"Help! Call 911! Help!"

Mimi Carter, the general manager of *Mallard Cove*'s food and beverage operations, was the only one at the restaurant so far. She was startled to hear some madman trying to break in through the back door but slightly relieved to see that it wasn't some stranger—instead, it was her friend Sandy Morgan. But the look on his face and the blood on his hands instantly erased any relief she'd felt. She quickly unlocked the door.

"Mimi, call 911! Bill and Betty have been attacked on *My Mahi*, and Bill's dying. We need paramedics now!"

"Oh my God, I'll call right away! How is Betty?"

He paused a split second, then replied, "Betty's dead, Mimi. But we have to save Bill."

1

FAMILY MATTERS

Thursday afternoon aboard *My Mahi...*

"I'M NOT crazy about the idea, Betty."

"Yes, but our niece is crazy about you, Bill. She moved down from Jersey and took that job in Hampton partly because you were close by; she wants to spend some time with her favorite and most famous uncle."

Betty Cooper smiled at her husband of several decades. Both were New Jersey natives who had migrated south to Virginia's Eastern Shore over twenty years ago. Now her sister's daughter had moved down as well, though she lived across the Chesapeake Bay Bridge-Tunnel (CBBT) over in the Tidewater area.

Captain Bill "Baloney" Cooper was just past sixty years old, the same age as Betty, though she was an inch taller than he at five-foot-six. Bill was mostly bald except for a strip of short salt-and-pepper-colored hair that circled halfway around his head just above his ears. Unlike soft-spoken Betty, Bill was usually loud, with a thick New Jersey accent he believed he'd lost years ago.

Most of the time, an unlit cigar stuck out of the corner of Bill's mouth. This was kind of an organic barometer of his current temperament. When he was agitated, it moved quickly from one side of his mouth to the other, seemingly unaided. This quirk was another part of why he'd become the most popular captain on the highly-rated cable show *Tuna Hunters*, a job that now earned him somewhere in the low seven figures annually. His unlit stogie had quickly become kind of a trademark; he only lit up when his boat cleared the mouth of the marina basin's inlet. This was a rule that Betty had instituted years ago—no smoking until then.

"I still don't like it, havin' ta run that old Chris Craft on a booze cruise for her sleazy boss. I mean, what kinda guy buys an old boat that size an' don't know how ta run it? Or any kinda boat? And he's too dang cheap ta hire a captain. He just parked it here because of all the young gals that come ta party at the bars on weekends. An' that name, *Oar House*, sounds close ta what he's tryin' ta turn it inta. That's another reason I don't like him bein' around Debbie."

"She's a big girl, Bill. She can handle herself."

"He's a sleaze, an' I don't trust him."

"Well, then, the good thing is you'll be around to keep an eye out for her." She smiled at him, bringing an end to the discussion. That smile was something he still adored about her after all their years together.

Their moment was interrupted by someone knocking on the side of the wheelhouse. They heard a muffled voice say, "Hey, Gilligan, c'mon! You wanted to catch up, and I'm going to let you buy me a beer at the bar."

Bill opened the door to the cockpit and stuck his head out. "I told ya ta quit callin' me that, ya hack! An' if anybody is gonna be buyin' beer around here, it's you! But we got an errand ta run first."

"Okay, fine, whatever. Let's go." Even the tone of Sandy Morgan's voice said clearly that he had no intention of picking up the tab. But then again, he never did. It became a battle of wits between the two over who got stuck paying.

The pair climbed into Bill's new pickup truck, and he drove them out of the marina parking lot. "I got a surprise ta show ya over at Carlton's." Carlton was Carlton Albury, the owner of *Albury's Boat Works*, a repair facility a couple of miles north of *Mallard Cove*.

"Whatever. So long as we're back soon enough to get a table at the *Cove Beach Bar*." The lunch crowd tended to be a large one, making tables scarce for those that arrive late.

"Keep yer shirt on, ya hack. I'll get us back in plenty ah time for ya ta pick up the beer an' the lunch tab."

"In your dreams, tuna boy. So, what's so important that it's coming between me and a free beer right now?"

Baloney smiled widely as he stared ahead. "You'll see."

FIVE MINUTES LATER, they pulled up next to a large, enclosed boat shed at *Albury's*. Baloney led Sandy through the side door and back to the stern of a sixty-foot Merritt sport fisherman that was blocked up inside the shed. The varnished teak transom bore the name *Dorado* in large, gold leaf letters, with the smaller hailing port of *Mallard Cove, VA*, underneath.

"Wow, she's coming out great, Bill." The sincerity in Sandy's voice was compounded by his using Baloney's given name. "The new name's clever—dolphin, only done in Spanish. And they're doing such a great job on her. You'd never know she'd been through a fire. But you're leaving the varnished stern? I thought you'd go with paint since it's easier to keep on a charter boat that gets hooks and sinkers bouncing off it by amateur anglers. Varnish can get ugly pretty fast in that environment."

"Yeah, well, that's if she was gonna be a charter boat. Wait'll ya see the interior." Baloney motioned for Sandy to go up a wooden stairway.

Dorado was the ex-*Irish Luck*, which had been owned and finally sold by Michael "Murph" and Lindsay Murphy, the majority owners of *Mallard Cove*.

The next owner had turned out to be a criminal. As a result, the boat had been burned by Murph, who used the fire as a distraction as well as partial revenge for a theft orchestrated by the man. The boat was subsequently seized by the government and auctioned last fall. Baloney had been the sole bidder, getting her for next to nothing.

Over the winter, *Albury's* had cut away and rebuilt the destroyed wheelhouse and flying bridge, and their replacements were now in the process of being prepped for painting.

As the pair walked inside, Sandy was taken aback at all the varnished wood veneer interior, which had been brought back to Merritt's original high standards.

"I thought you were going to do a painted interior like you did when you rebuilt *My Mahi*."

"Nah, like I said, this ain't gonna be a charter boat. I want her lookin' as good as she can. I'm gonna spring her on Betty as our new home."

"Nice! A lot more room than in *My Mahi*."

"Yep. I think she's gonna like it."

"I'd say that's a pretty safe bet, Gilligan."

It was the first time that Sandy ever saw him smile after being called by that name.

As THE PAIR walked down the covered walkway between *Mallard Cove's* two beach bars, Sandy said, "Today's your lucky day, Gilligan. I'm suddenly feeling generous, and I've decided I will pick up our tab... at the '*Cat*.'"

Baloney briefly scowled at the repeated mention of his despised nickname before quickly smiling at Sandy's offer. Then the smile vanished as quickly as it had appeared as the catch that came with it dawned on him. "Yer not serious!"

"It's as generous an offer as I've ever made, so yes, I'm serious."

"Nah, that wasn't a question. I mean, ya can't seriously think I'd go in there again, right? Buncha dadgum blow-boaters!"

The "*Cat*" was short for the *Catamaran Beach Bar*, which had been built to accommodate the local sailing crowd, the "blow-boaters" to which Baloney referred. It was on the left side of the covered walkway, directly across from the adjacent *Mallard Cove Beach Bar*, which was the preferred watering hole for the sportfishing and powerboat crowd.

Over the past two years since they built the *Catamaran*, you could count on one hand the number of times that Baloney had darkened its door. Not that it even had a door. Both bars were basically of the same layout and construction: open-air with large wood pilings and beams supporting corrugated galvanized steel roofs. Each had a rectangular bar in the center, surrounded by a sea of tables and chairs. The only differences between the two were their styles of seating and decor.

The *Cove's* bar was equipped with standard barstools, while the *Cat* had two long fiberglass benches alongside its bar. These were made from the hulls of a prototype racing catamaran. The sails from that experimental boat were attached to the wooden beams overhead.

"You can't say I never offered, Gilligan. So, since you're turning me down, that must mean that now it's your turn to pick up the tab at the *Cove*."

"In yer dreams, Hack. And what's this 'turn' stuff? I never agreed ta that!" He turned into his preferred bar, making a beeline for a table that had just opened up. It was one of his favorites, located over by the edge of the concrete floor where it abutted the beach. Sandy followed, taking a seat across from him.

Their server, Angel, approached the table. "Good afternoon, fellas. What'll it be? Not that I really have to ask." She was well acquainted with their favorites. Sandy always went for a Jamaican Red Stripe, while Baloney ordered the cheapest of whatever was on draft unless he was certain that he could stick someone else with the tab, then he'd go with the more expensive Bahamian Kalik.

Baloney grinned. "The hack there is buyin'."

"In your dreams, Gilligan!"

"Never mind him, gimme the good stuff."

Angel chuckled. "One Red Stripe and one Kalik, coming right up."

Sandy frowned. "I meant it."

"Yeah, me too. But we can worry about that later. I wanna talk to ya about somethin'. You been ta London, right?"

Sandy nodded. "Yes, though it was years ago. My late wife and I took our dream trip to Europe after my first book got made into a movie, and that check went into the bank. I was able to pay off all my debts, and for the first time in our lives, we weren't stressed over money. I'm so happy that we had so many good years with some great times before she got sick. Not that we didn't have any fun when we were just scraping by, but we were finally able to cross off a lot of 'bucket list' items in the last few years of her life."

"That's what I'm talkin' about! My gig on *Tuna Hunters* has made me enough ta pay off all the boats an' pay for the work that's goin' inta *Dorado*. I even stashed a bunch in the bank an' the stock market. Me'n Betty both started IRAs, too. We finally hit that point yer talkin' about. I don't hafta take out another charter if I don't wanna, or even do another season on the show, an' we could still retire. But I'm gonna stay on the show so long as it's still fun ta do it. I got life by the ass."

Baloney paused as Angel returned with their beers. They each took a healthy swig from the bottles before Baloney continued.

"Anyway, we got enough left over now, even before the fall filming season, that I wanna start doin' some ah that 'bucket list' stuff like you said. Betty held down a job alla those years before I got on the show, workin' her tail off so we could build our charter business. I'd ah had ta go ta work for somebody if she hadn't. An' now that we can afford it, I wanna show her I appreciate what she did. All that time, she dreamed ah goin' ta England. An' now we can."

Sandy leaned back in his chair, studying his friend's face. This was the first time that Bill had opened up and been completely serious with him. No bluster, no jabs, just him being Bill Cooper and showing his true core. Of course, Sandy had known who he was inside all along; he didn't become a bestselling novelist without knowing a lot about people, even the parts they like to keep hidden from the world.

"You're a good man, Bill Cooper. And a trip to London for you two is a great way to show how much you appreciate her and all she's done to support your shared dream. Everyone needs to have a dream, but it's only the lucky few that get to achieve them. I'm glad that's come true for you guys; you'll have a ball over there. But don't just stay in London, get out into the countryside. It's so beautiful and less crowded."

"Yeah, that's the one thing I'm not lookin' forward to is big city crowds. I don't even like goin' ta Virginia Beach unless I hafta. But I'm springin' for first-class seats on the plane, so at least that part won't be crowded."

Sandy grinned. "You get free beer in the front of the plane, too."

Baloney matched his grin, "Yeah, ain't it great? Almost as good as you pickin' up the tab today!"

"Hah! Another one of your dreams. Good thing the other one came true. One out of two isn't bad."

"Oh yeah? We'll see about that."

"Speaking about dreams, isn't that one of your dream boats?" Sandy pointed over Baloney's shoulder toward Fisherman Inlet Bridge.

Baloney turned around and spotted the vintage sixty-five-foot Chesapeake buyboat. Those classic workboats were a favorite with Baloney. Turning back to Sandy, he was frowning. "Yeah, I know that one, the *Sandra T.* Those Ko-reeans musta got all the bugs outa th' system an' went ahead an' splashed her. Ya ask me, that's nuts, putin' an electric motor an' a buncha lithium batteries in her. Ya know what happens if those batteries crack an' get water inside 'em? Bye-bye, buyboat. Poof, instant Ko-reean barbecue. Hard as hell ta put it out, too."

"Korean barbecue? Lithium batteries?"

"The guy who owns her is a Korean, an' he just dropped a ton ah money on her over at *Albury's* doin' th' engine swap. Hadta cut a bigger hatch over th' hold ta fit th' batteries, too. Waste ah money if ya ask me.

"Nah, gimme a good diesel any day. All this green electric stuff is gettin' shoved down our throats 'cause a buncha politicians and their donor buddies are set ta make a fortune off it. Mark my words, nothin' good'll come outta it in the long run. Crazy ta have lithium batteries around salt water anyway. They burp hydrogen an' pee acid when it gets inta 'em. Not ta mention the seven-hundred volts electrocutin' everything an' everybody in th' water aroun' it.

"Remember that hurricane in Florida last year that flooded Naples? Two dozen ah those electric cars that got flooded caught fire over th' next two weeks. They get 'em all put out, and some of 'em caught fire again the next day. Nope, you'll never catch me around one ah those things."

Sandy chuckled. "Don't hold back there, Gilligan; tell me how you really feel."

Baloney ignored the jibe. "Oughta be a law against screwin' up ah piece ah history like that great ol' boat."

The *Sandra T* had passed out of sight behind *Mallard Cove's Driftwood Stage* building on the beach but now reappeared opposite them just beyond the venue. She continued on her course, passing by a hundred yards off the beach.

"I don't know how screwed up it is, Gilligan. She looks like she's standing pretty tall. New paint and even varnished trim. Not something you see every day on a workboat."

"That's what I'm talkin' about, ya hack! A real buyboat has got painted trim, if it's got any trim at all, and it ain't varnished." Baloney almost spat out the word *varnished*.

"If you want to get right down to it, Gilligan, back in the early part of the twentieth century, most of them had sails and no deck, just a huge open hold. They've changed a lot since then, so maybe electric power is another logical progression in their design history."

"Says you." He signaled Angel for another beer. "I guess you're a fan ah turnin' them into booze cruisers, too." He scowled at Sandy.

"Better that than breaking them up, don't you think?"

"I think I'd rather see 'em stay as workboats. There's somethin' so wrong about makin' 'em into pleasure boats. Only a few left these days anyway." He upended his bottle, finishing off this first beer.

Chesapeake buyboats were another workboat design whose time and need had mostly come and gone. They had high bows with low rails amidship. Tall wood masts on their bows with stout booms facilitated the loading and unloading of cargo from their holds and off their decks. Small wheelhouses with round fronts were located aft. These were similar to the wheelhouses still being built today on smaller tugboats. This helped make the buyboats' profiles unmistakable, even at a distance.

Back in the days of muddy, rutted roads, these boats were the floating semi-trucks that delivered everything from lumber and supplies all around the Chesapeake much faster than what could happen by land. Then they picked up produce and seafood to be hauled back across the bay to markets in the larger towns on the western shore. Eventually, the open-hulled designs gave way to those enclosed decks, hence the name "deck boats." Cargoes like fish and produce could then be stowed out of the sun down in the hold, while other goods, such as lumber, could be stacked outside on the deck.

As land transportation conditions improved, the need for hauling freight by deck boats began to disappear. Their captains switched their focus to concentrate on buying the catches from smaller boats that worked locally. Those local fishing captains learned that selling wholesale to these larger buyboats allowed them to stay out longer, concentrating on increasing the day's catch rather than having to cross the bay once their boats reached capacity. More time spent fishing meant more money, enough to more than offset the lower wholesale prices. The deck boats would load up with the catches from several smaller fishing boats, then make their runs to Baltimore, Norfolk, Annapolis, and other large towns where they sold their goods at retail prices at the wharves.

Another use for buyboats was to build and tend the large, deep water "pound nets." These were basically huge fish traps constructed of netting and wooden pilings that were positioned both in shallow water and the deeper water out in the bay. Smaller skiffs generally tended the ones in the shallows, but it took these larger buyboats to be able to haul and set the longer pilings needed for fishing the bay's deeper water.

But as the need for these classic boats diminished, they began to disappear. A few still ply the bay today as workboats, but many have been repurposed, as Baloney mentioned, becoming pleasure craft.

Baloney watched the *Sandra T* as it passed the inlet for *Mallard Cove Marina's* basin and continued on into the narrow channel of the *Virginia Inside Passage*. "Looks like it's goin' back ta *Albury's*. Probably got problems with that crazy motor setup."

"Or, he's enjoying a nice, quiet cruise out on such a beautiful day," Sandy countered.

Baloney's eyes narrowed. "What? Sounds like you like what they did. Don't tell me yer thinkin' about doin' that ta *Epilogue!*"

"I didn't say that; I merely suggested that he might be out enjoying a cruise on his boat. I have half a mind to do the same since anything would be better than listening to you bitch and moan all afternoon." He stopped and looked thoughtful before continuing, "But we were having such a nice conversation before about..."

Baloney interrupted, "Look at that! There's one you'll like." He pointed to the south, where a vintage fifty-three-foot Hatteras yacht-fisherman was about three hundred yards out on a course for the marina. It was towing a dark blue, twin-outboard Scarab that was just over half the length of the Hatteras.

Sandy turned and looked in the direction Baloney had indicated. "You're right about that one, Gilligan. Much more up my alley. She's been taken care of, too. Nice to see that. And look, she's Bahamian registered." He had spotted the large, blue, and yellow-striped flag with its black triangle flying proudly from the back of the flybridge deck.

As they watched, the Hatteras slowed, and a man appeared in the cockpit, pulling in the tow line. Once the Scarab was close enough, he clambered aboard, untying and tossing the rest of the line onto the

Hatteras. The Scarab then maneuvered around its mothership and sped ahead of it into the marina.

Sandy nodded his approval. "Scarab tender. Classy. Both of those boats look like new."

"They're a long way from home," Baloney noted.

"They are indeed, but the Bahamas are a lot hotter than here right now. This is a great place to be in the summer." He turned back to his friend. "Though England isn't too bad, either."

2

THE INVENTOR

Eric Cottell eased his Hatteras, *Providence*, in and out of gear, stalling for time just outside of *Mallard Cove Marina's* basin until Tommy, his mate, finished docking the Scarab. Once he saw him tie up at the floating dock, Eric expertly maneuvered *Providence* in and around the "tee" end. Then he used both his throttles and gears to slide her into the slip next to the Scarab. At idle speed, the rudders had less effect than the boat's large propellers, so he had centered the rudders amidship and now all but ignored the wheel.

Tommy jumped back aboard and made his way forward, where he had dock lines already prepped and waiting. With the help of the dockmaster, the two tied a bow, spring, and stern line to the cleats on the floating finger pier. As he made his way aft, he adjusted the large, rubbery plastic fenders so that they were positioned between the hull and the dock, preventing chafing of the hull.

Eric shut down both engines and climbed down from the flybridge, stepping over onto the finger pier where the dockmaster was waiting. He offered his hand. "I'm Eric."

The dockmaster shook it and said, "Barry. I don't see many of those around here." He indicated the Bahamian flag. "You're a long way from home."

"Unless I miss my guess, I'd say it sounds like you are as well. New Providence or Grand Bahama?"

Barry grinned and replied, "Neither. Born in Abaco, on Grand Cay." He pronounced the word *cay* as *key*, the typical Bahamian pronunciation.

Eric nodded. "It's been a while, but I've been to Grand a few times. Good fishing and great diving."

"It's what we're best known for. But I think you'll like it here, too. We've got your reservation down as staying for two weeks."

"Yes, but it may be a bit longer, I don't know. Would that be a problem?"

"Not at all. We can extend your stay as long as you need. Just let me know, Cap'n."

"Thanks." Eric turned to Tommy. "No need to soap the 'bridge, just the foredeck and the cockpit, and then rinse the hull. It was so calm we didn't take hardly any spray. But give the Scarab a total wash."

Tommy nodded. "Got it, Eric."

Barry said, "I almost forgot, a couple of boxes came for you; they're up at the dockmaster's office. Kinda heavy."

"Oh, good, I was hoping they'd beat us here. I'll grab a quick bite and then be 'round to pick them up. Where's the best place for lunch and a beer?"

"Either the *Cove Restaurant* or the *Beach Bar*. Pretty much the same food—it all comes out of the same kitchen. Oh, an' they got Kalik beer, too!"

"*Beach Bar* it is then, thanks." He turned back to his mate. "You can wash everything after we have lunch. Come on; I'll buy."

As the pair entered the open-air bar, Eric spotted an empty two-top next to the far corner, one table away from the beach. As they sat down, they couldn't help but overhear the argument that was happening at an adjacent table. Two men were debating the benefits of different types of engine systems. Loudly. One of them had a very distinctive New Jersey accent and much higher-than-necessary volume.

"I'm tellin' ya, people are crazy if they think these over-priced, high-speed golf carts are anything but a fad! Th' pet rock of the two thousands. Ya can't charge 'em just anywhere, an' I can fill the gas tank in my pickup from empty much faster than the fastest charger can top off one ah those things. Oh, an' ya can forget about takin' a long trip in one of 'em. Just wait'll the next hurricane down in Florida, an' the interstates get backed up like they always do. There'll be a ton of dead batteries from people sittin' still, usin' their A/Cs ta keep 'em from fryin'.

"An' now they wanna make outboards electric? I just saw a new one out in a magazine that said it'll run for two hours without a charge. Two hours? Are ya freakin' kiddin' me? That'll barely get ya out ta the canyons ta fish on a flat-calm day! Then how're ya supposed ta get home?

"An' I don't know where they think all ah that juice comes from; I hear sixty percent is straight from coal an' gas. Only fifteen percent comes from solar an' wind. Start suckin' more outa th' grid, an' just where do they expect it ta come from? Maybe put more windmills in DC, an' then we can finally get somethin' useful outta all that hot air from those blowhards in Congress."

Sandy tilted his head slightly. "I have to say, I'm impressed, Gilligan. Your numbers line up with what I've read, too. And I agree there are a lot of questions surrounding what the government is trying to force us into and not a lot of good explanations coming out of Washington. The strain on the grid, questionable battery life, no proper disposal procedures, not to mention the fire dangers involved. But don't forget, gas boats originally had their dangers, too."

Baloney snorted. "Yeah, but we figured out how ta deal with those, didn't we? An' there's gotta be a better way ta deal with what we already got, instead ah scrappin' the whole thing an' startin' over. We need ta make stuff cleaner without breakin' the bank over it."

"Ahem." One of the two guys that had sat down next to them cleared his throat to get their attention. It worked. A quick glance was all they needed to tell he was someone who spent a lot of time around the water. It wasn't just about his deep tan or the sun creases on his face, or his sun-lightened hair. It was also about the SPF-rated fishing shirt he wore and the Croakies attached to both pairs of glasses—one clear pair on his face and the other with polarized lenses dangling down the front of his shirt.

"I'm sorry, I couldn't help but overhear your conversation, and you're both right. If this is truly about emissions, then why not focus on improving those instead of chucking the whole system that took a century to put in place and perfect? It makes no sense to abandon the existing process and fuel supply line without trying to fix it first. Look at the tighter regulations they've already put in place for marine engines. Manufacturers are stepping up and meeting those. And there are systems out there that exist or are coming online that can further significantly reduce emissions."

Baloney scowled. "Yeah, pal, you're right; this is *our* conversation. Why don't ya stick ta orderin' yer lunch an' butt out."

Sandy had been studying the guy and trying to place his slight accent. He decided it was part Bahamian, with maybe some UK English and a bit of northeastern US influence. He was obviously well-educated. "Wait a minute, Gilligan, let's hear what the man has to say. By the way, was that your Hatteras that pulled in a while ago?"

Eric nodded. "Yes, that's *Providence*. I'm Eric Cottell, and this is Tommy, my mate," he nodded toward the young man across the table from him. "I'm president of Nonox Limited. We manufacture a system that combines fuel and water to create an emulsion that burns much cleaner than fuel alone."

Baloney rolled his eyes. "The last thing I want is water in my diesel."

"If it were dumped straight into your fuel tank, you'd be right. But as I was saying, the Nonox system I invented incorporates those two liquids to form an emulsion just before it is introduced into the fuel system of an engine or a boiler. It binds the two liquids together. This cuts different emission gasses like nitrogen oxides by up to fifty percent and particulate matter by up to ninety percent, all while reducing fuel consumption by as much as fifteen percent. So, it adds up to less fuel consumption combined with a much cleaner exhaust."

"What's 'particulate matter'?" Baloney asked.

"That black, stinky cloud of carbon that both of your boats belch out when you crank them up or hit the throttles," Sandy replied. "You might try listening to the man, and then maybe you can quit gassing us all out every morning." He turned to Eric. "So, why haven't we heard more about this Nonox thing before?"

"It's not for lack of trying, I can assure you. And we do have some units in boilers in large buildings in New York, along with a few freighters and cruise ships. But it has been tough to get widespread attention. If it isn't about improving electric propulsion, Washington is turning a deaf ear to it. They want to kill off anything to do with fossil fuels, even if it makes them more environmentally friendly.

"And a lot of people have the same reaction as your friend here, believing water and fuel don't mix. But they do with my system, and the fuel emulsion is so much less taxing on engines, helping them by also extending their working life. So now I'm working on a smaller-scale unit for boats like *Providence*, hoping this will help us find a wider, more accepting audience."

Sandy asked, "Why here at *Mallard Cove*? It seems like an out-of-the-way place to do that kind of work."

"Exactly the point. Fewer people looking over my shoulder while I work. Yet it's a lot easier to find the generic parts that I need here through suppliers to the naval yards. In addition, we have a production facility here in Virginia, in Edinburg, that can make any custom fabricated parts and get them to me in a few hours.

"The import duties over in the Bahamas are steep, not to mention the headaches involved in the logistics of getting things shipped over and passed through Customs. Plus, I had seen *Mallard Cove* online and talked to a few boaters back at my home dock in Nassau that have been here and loved this place. So, I'm mixing a bit of business with pleasure while I perfect my smaller-scale unit."

"Ohhh, I get it now." Baloney looked at Sandy. "This guy is here ta try an' talk me inta puttin' one ah these things on my boat so I can endorse it, an' show it off on *Tuna Hunters*. Well, that ain't gonna happen, fella."

Eric looked confused. "Why would I want you to endorse my invention? Who are you, and what is *Tuna Hunters*?"

Sandy smiled, knowing what was about to happen. He could see the color starting to rise in Baloney's cheeks.

"Yeah, like you don't already know. I'm Captain Bill Cooper, th' star of th' highest-rated show on cable, *Tuna Hunters*. An' there's no way I'm gonna endorse your snake oil, no matter how much ya wanna pay me."

"I'm sorry, I've never heard of you or your show, so I don't think I'll be advertising with you anytime soon."

"Yeah, sure. An' I suppose ya never heard ah my buddy here, either." He looked at Sandy again. "This whole thing is some kinda setup."

"Your friend never introduced himself, so how would I know who he is? And I thought your friend called you Gilligan."

"*NO!* My name's not Gilligan!" He glared at Sandy before looking back at Eric. "And oh right, like ya never saw his picture on his books. So ya don't know he's Sanford Morgan." Baloney rolled his eyes again.

"Ah yes, Sanford Morgan, the novelist! I do recognize you now. Nice to meet you."

"Likewise, but call me Sandy. And any thorn in Gilligan's side is a friend of mine!" Sandy grinned, seeing how red Baloney's face had become.

"I'll let you two get back to your chat, but feel free to stop by my boat around cocktail hour if you'd like. We can sit and talk a bit more over a drink or two in a much quieter environment." Eric hesitated, then added as he looked at Baloney, "Both of you. It might prove to be an interesting conversation."

IT WAS JUST BEFORE five o'clock, and the two men were walking down the dock where Eric's two boats were tied up. Coincidentally, it was also the same dock where Baloney's niece's boss kept his aging, new-to-him Chris Craft Constellation. As they passed by it, Baloney scowled. It was all too obvious that the previous owner hadn't been much into boat maintenance, and as Baloney had already noted, the new one also liked to sit on his wallet.

Baloney asked, "Tell me again why we're goin' ta this guy's boat?"

Sandy replied, "I'm going because I think he's interesting. I want to know more about this emulsion thing he's working on, and he was kind enough to extend an invitation to me in spite of my having sat and put up with you while you were being such a jerk. You were only invited because he has better manners than you do."

"Yeah, well, my manners're good enough to show up for some free beer."

Sandy had noticed Baloney's scowl as they passed an older Chris Craft. He said, "Right, we're closing in on some free beer. So, what's eating you? I thought you'd be happy."

Baloney jerked his thumb back toward *Oar House*, "See that piece of floatin' crap back there? Belongs to my niece's boss, an' I got roped inta runnin' it on a booze cruise tomorra night. Th' guy don't know how, an' I don't want him playin' pinball wizard in my marina, bouncin' offa my boats. Figured I'd start teachin' him how ta run the boat an' dock the right way, usin' just the gears an' stayin' away from the throttles. He's got so much ta learn, but he's one ah those young, hotshot, know-it-all, wanna-be-corporate CEO types. If I didn't love my niece so much, I'd have told him ta take a walk already." He sighed deeply before adding, "The things we do for family, ya know?"

"You're a good man, Bill Cooper."

"Yeah, I know. Just don't spread it around; it'd ruin my image. An' that's *Captain* Bill Cooper, ya hack."

"Whatever you say, Gilligan."

∽

"FUNNY HOW PEOPLE come around from other faraway places that you know when you're on the water." Over the past hour and a half, Sandy learned that he and Eric Cottell had several friends and acquaintances in common. While this was going on, Baloney had concentrated on becoming acquainted with a few more of Eric's beers while the trio sat on *Providence*'s raised aft deck.

Eric nodded. "Lots of the same boats that visit the Keys also come to the Bahamas, so it's not that unusual. I've been in your store twice as well, Sandy, though I don't recall seeing you when I was there."

"My ex-store. I was probably out, guiding one of my clients the times you came in. I tried getting on the water as often as I could. Sitting the store wasn't my favorite thing to do. Can't say that I miss the retail part of my life history."

Sandy had started out as a guide in Islamorada, in the Florida Keys, before opening up an outfitter shop there. He passed the business to his long-time shop manager right before leaving the Keys for good when he moved his boat up to *Mallard Cove*. He'd only been back down to visit once in the past two years.

Baloney raised his bottle in a salute. "Much better havin' ya around here than down there anyways."

"Thanks, Baloney."

"Yeah, it would be real hard ta stick ya with the bar tab long-distance!" Baloney laughed at his own joke.

Sandy asked, "Where's your mate, Eric?"

"Ah, I think Tommy is trying to get to know that pretty brunette bartender at the beach bar. We were pushing hard to get up here, so I'm taking it easy on him the next few days, letting him take some time for himself in the afternoons."

"Nice of you." Sandy turned to watch a boat that was coming into the marina. "Hey Gilligan, isn't that your favorite boat?"

"I told ya ta quit callin' me that!" He looked in the direction Sandy had indicated and saw it was indeed the *Sandra T*, now silently passing *Providence* and turning bow first into the slip just beyond Eric's Scarab. Two Asian-looking crewmen in khaki uniforms stood by with dock lines as the boat slowed and pulled in alongside a floating finger pier.

"So weird, not having any engine or transmission noise," Sandy commented. "Though it's nice, too."

"Ya mean it's wrong. Workboats are supposed ta make noise; if they ain't, they're broke," Baloney said.

Eric commented, "It appears to me that this one's working days are long past. That's a pretty nice setup with those teak decks and the long bench seats with the canvas tent sunshade. Really comfortable and elegant for day cruises with a lot of people."

"That's part ah what I'm talkin' about! I've never seen one with teak decks before. Turned the darn thing into a fancy tourist hauler. A damn pimp ship."

Baloney then upended his beer bottle, finishing it and reaching for another. "This'll have ta be my last brew, I gotta look that damn Chris over tonight an' see if I need ta fix anything tomorra before I take those kids on that sunset cruise." He had already explained to Eric about his upcoming favor to his niece.

"Nice of you, Baloney. Not just taking her friends out, but being here for her in general," Eric said. "Must be comforting to her after taking that leap of faith by moving to Virginia."

"Yeah, I guess so, Gizmo."

"Gizmo?" Eric looked confused.

"Yeah, that's your new nickname, 'cause ah yer fuel gizmo thing." A sly smile spread across Baloney's face.

Eric looked at Sandy with an almost pleading face, but he was met with a smile instead of his hoped-for help. Sandy shook his head and made downward motions with both hands, silently suggesting that he relax.

Baloney raised his new beer and said, "Well, I gotta take this one for the walk down the dock so I can check that rig over while it's still light out." He tilted his head, looking thoughtful. "Ya know, Giz, maybe tomorra I'll let you show me that fuel-saver exhaust-scrubber thingy."

Slightly thrown by the now shortened "Giz," Eric paused for a brief second before responding, "It's not an exhaust scrubber! Those things dump tons of carcinogens into the oceans. The Nonox system's emulsion prevents engines and boilers from making those pollutants in the first place, eliminating the need for scrubbers and preventing that kind of ocean pollution."

"Yeah, whatever. But ya say it'll save me up ta fifteen percent of my fuel?"

"Yes, depending on what engines you have."

"Huh. Well, that'll be worth lookin' at. If it ain't snake oil, mebbe I might letcha put 'em on my rigs after all. We'll see. Anyway, g'night there, Hack. G'night, Giz." He pulled a fresh cigar out of his top pocket and stuck it in his mouth before climbing down into the fishing cockpit and then over onto the dock.

Once Baloney was out of earshot, Eric said to Sandy, "Gizmo? Really?"

Sandy chuckled. "You should feel honored. He only gives nicknames to people he likes and thinks are interesting."

Eric retorted, "And those who have a stock of cold beer on hand."

"Well, yes, there is that. Speaking of which, would you mind..."

"Help yourself." He motioned to the cooler. "I thought I might have to exchange some Bahamian dollars for US, but it appears that the official currency of *Mallard Cove* might instead be beer."

Sandy chuckled again. "Pretty much."

BALONEY PAUSED at the bow of the *Sandra T*, looking her over. One of the Asian crewmen came out of the wheelhouse and walked up to the bow. "You no board."

"Cool yer jets, I'm just lookin'."

The man repeated, "You no board."

"I ain't about ta!" Baloney's volume increased as he wasn't used to having someone tell him what he could or couldn't do.

Another man stepped out of the wheelhouse and spoke sharply to the crewman in a language Baloney didn't understand. Unlike the uniformed crewman, this man was dressed in a light-colored polo-style shirt with dark pants and boat shoes. He came up to the bow as the crewman retreated.

In slightly accented English, he said, "I apologize if my man was rude. The teak was recently oiled, so I am not allowing anyone but my crew aboard right now." He continued, "My name is DaeSeong Han, and I am the owner. I saw you admiring my yacht and wanted to introduce myself."

"Admiring? Yacht?" Baloney's cigar was now moving rapidly from side to side in his mouth. "Mister, ya took a great piece ah Chesapeake history an' ruined it. A buyboat is supposed ta look like the workboat it was built as, not some fancy pimp rig."

Han looked like he'd been slapped across his face. "Ruined? I save this hull from scrapyard. With my new electric propulsion system, this will last far into next century! This the future, and you are stuck in past." His facial features were definitely Asian, and as his temper rose, his accent became more pronounced and his speech much less refined.

"Oh, yeah? Well, I'd rather live in the past than hafta deal with all this electric stuff that'll be a pile ah corroded garbage inside a year. Buyboats should have diesel engines. An' ya wanna look at the real future? It's all about that water an' diesel emulsion gizmo they're tinkerin' with on that Hatteras over there. Uses fifteen percent less fuel an' runs better an' cleaner. That's the real future, not some electric junk."

Baloney turned on his heel, heading for the Chris Craft. Han watched him go, not surprised that he was involved with such a floating derelict. He thought to himself *If he only knew about the real reason behind my electric drive. Hah!*

BACK ABOARD *PROVIDENCE*, Eric, and Sandy had overheard the confrontation between Baloney and the owner of the buyboat. They were almost a hundred feet away, but both men's voices had become louder as they argued.

Eric looked incredulous. "Did I just hear that right? Did your friend just refer to my Nonox system as the future? He seemed to dismiss the idea earlier."

"I think you can thank the buyboat guy for that. Baloney loves taking sides, and he just got shoved way over onto yours. I think you're going to need two more of your units for the *Golden Dolphin*. If they work as well as you say they do, you couldn't ask for a better demo platform. Not to mention, Baloney's big mouth can be a plus, especially when he starts chatting with the other charter crews on his VHF radio."

Eric laughed. "With his apparently normal volume, he doesn't need the radio."

3

———

OAR HOUSE

O nce aboard *Oar House*, Baloney began by inspecting the engine room. The boat's aging Detroit Diesel engines appeared to have seen better days. Sheet metal trays in the sumps beneath the two engines prevented any leaking oil from getting into the bilge and then being pumped overboard by the automatic bilge pumps. Usually, this was enough of a barrier between engines and the marine environment. But these old engines were leaking steadily around their aging gaskets and seals, so someone had placed disposable diapers in the trays under each of them as an added precaution. Those were now completely saturated with very used, very black oil that was well overdue for a change. The same was true for the vintage diesel generator.

When Baloney pulled the dipsticks, not surprisingly, the engines were low. The oil looked like it hadn't been changed in forever; again, not much of a surprise. When engines get this "run-out" and leak this badly, oftentimes, oil only gets added instead of changed. This also meant that the filters probably hadn't been changed either and were likely clogged.

A glance around the engine room only added to his suspicions when he spotted a full and a half-empty case of oil in quarts, but there were no replacement oil filters in sight. When oil gets changed in such high-capacity, large diesels like this pair, it's usually pumped straight out of five-gallon containers, not quarts. This was the cheapest and easiest way to buy and handle that much oil in such tight quarters where the engine room ceiling height is less than four feet. The only reason to have so many smaller quarts of oil is to make continually adding to each engine easier since they're leaking so badly, as well as burning oil.

Baloney shook his head and muttered to himself as he wiped his hands and climbed up through the hatch, back up into the salon. Even during his busiest time in the season with continuous back-to-back charters, he'd never let either the *Golden Dolphin* or *My Mahi's* oil and engines get this bad. *Oar House's* engine room was a greasy, dark pigsty that had been ignored by her previous owners. Then again, he thought, why should that part of the boat be any different than the rest?

Looking around the salon, he saw how worn and decrepit it was. *Oar House* was what most lower-tier yacht brokers would typically describe as "the perfect liveaboard." Meaning that the boat is cheap and has plenty of living space. But this can also refer to the question of the hull's integrity, which in this case, was very questionable. Baloney wouldn't dare take *Oar House* out in anything but flat-calm seas. However, this wasn't just because of the hull; these old engines were likely at the end of their service life and were now living on borrowed time.

With the low value of these older boats, replacing the engines was akin to replacing the batteries in an aging Chevy Volt; it would cost you way more than its overall value after the transplant. Fortunately, most older liveaboards tended to stay tied up at their docks, venturing out only when conditions were perfect or it became neces-sary. Which is what really should happen with this rig, Baloney thought to himself. Fortunately, or maybe unfortunately, the forecast for tomorrow night was "severe clear" with calm seas. He had no excuse in order to cancel.

After going up the short flight of stairs to the helm station,

Baloney cranked up the generator, followed by the engines. In the engine room, he'd noticed that the three sets of batteries were new. This was probably because they were replaced by the last owner to ensure they'd at least start for a sea trial. Both of the engines and the generator had cranked over easily. He turned and walked out onto the covered aft deck, where a cloud of black sooty exhaust from the Detroits was now moving away from the boat's stern and toward the main dock. Apparently, the engines' injectors were on the growing list of things that had also long been ignored and helped to create the carbon cloud.

"Hah! I thought you said your emulsion device makes your engines run cleaner." Han had been walking by on the dock and was now beginning to gag as the carbon cloud engulfed him.

Baloney scowled. "Not my device; that's Eric Cottell's." He pointed over at *Providence*. "And this ain't my boat; it's a friend of a friend's. I'm just doin' a favor, checking it over."

Baloney was mad for feeling the need to answer Han instead of ignoring him and then ending up in a position where he'd had to defend himself. Watching Han now walk away with a big, satisfied smirk on his face didn't help Baloney's temperament as he went back to inspecting the boat.

ABOARD *MY MAHI* a few minutes later, Baloney told Betty, "That scow's even worse'n I thought. Diapers under the engines, an' you can see all ah th' planks in the hull through cracks in th' paint. I think the hull's probably workin' pretty good."

This last remark wasn't a compliment; it referred to how the hull was weakening and beginning to flex. However, the thing about old wood-planked boats was that they could always be repaired. The question was whether it was worth the cost or not. When boats needed as much work as *Oar House*, the answer was usually "not."

"I've been thinking, Bill, it might be a good idea if I came along with you tomorrow. I doubt if any of the crowd he's inviting have much experience handling boats of that size, and I can help."

Baloney smiled. "I was hopin' ya'd offer. Misery loves company, ya know."

Betty nodded. "I'm guessing you aren't planning on going out too far."

"Nah. We'll keep it close ta shore. Maybe outside up along the barrier islands. I don't wanna run inside th' bay 'cause ah the pilings on those pound nets. The radar doesn't work, ah course, so we'd be runnin' blind. So, we'll stay a little offshore, just in case we run inta trouble. I just hope we don't end up swimmin'."

"That bad?"

He nodded. "Worse. Th' good news is it's got a decent life raft."

"Maybe we should cancel, Bill. I mean, if you don't think it's safe."

"You an' I been on worse, but not by much. I checked the bilge pumps an' they're all good. So, we'll just take it slow an' easy. I'll show the kid how ta pull her outta the slip without bouncin' off other boats an' how ta get her tied back up the same way."

"Tell you what, Bill, let's have dinner at the *Cove* tonight. We'll relax and let somebody else cook and clean up." Betty had seen how tense Baloney was and wanted to snap him out of his dour mood.

He nodded, "Sounds good ta me."

"Speaking of cleaning up, you need to shower and change. Those diapers aren't the only things that soaked up some oil."

FROM UP AT his table on the *Cove Restaurant*'s deck, Han had seen Baloney enter the salon on a mid-sized Viking sport fisherman named *My Mahi*. Now, half an hour later, he saw him emerge in fresh clothes and with a nice-looking woman about his age.

Apparently, he'd been telling the truth about that Chris Craft not being his. This Viking must be his and the woman's home. The man was such an ignorant fool, boasting about the device his friend was working on. The electric propulsion system Han installed in the buyboat was so far advanced from most of today's marine electric drives and necessary for the task ahead. But he wanted to find out more about this emulsion device. What the man said about it using so much less fuel was intriguing; he wanted more specifics. He wasn't concerned with the pollution reduction part of the equation. But any fuel savings for his homeland would be a huge benefit since North Korea had to import all of its oil-based products. Sanctions put in place by the United Nations had put tight restrictions on the amount they were allowed to import annually.

Recently, the UN discovered North Korea was covertly smuggling large quantities of petroleum products into the country that weren't being declared under the sanctions. This caused even more trouble for Han's government. Or rather, for his employer, since he no longer saw himself as a subject of that regime but rather as an independent contractor. He had no intention of returning to North Korea permanently after this current job was completed.

If, and that was a big *if*, this device proved to be as promising as the man claimed, it could be worth a fortune to the country's current leadership. In that case, stealing the technology was worth whatever risk he had to run. He didn't care about any patents that might be covering the device. In North Korea, the patents of other countries were more valuable as toilet paper when wadded up and converted to a softer consistency. Han was now determined to find out all about the device, even if it meant having to befriend the coarse dolt who was now sitting four tables away from him. He might need him to make an introduction to this Cottell person if Han wasn't able to befriend the man by himself.

Han signaled for his server to come over and told him what he wanted. The man disappeared inside, and when he came back out, he was carrying a bottle of Kalik and a glass of wine on his tray. He set the drinks in front of Baloney and Betty, then pointed over at Han, who bowed slightly. Baloney glared in return. Han saw Betty say something to him, but he just scowled. She then put a hand on his arm. After this soft rebuke, he lifted the beer a couple of inches above the table and nodded curtly in Han's direction. Han briefly considered going over and talking to the couple but decided against it. With the man apparently living at *Mallard Cove* and having a connection to the old Chris Craft tied up near him, he'd probably be running into him on the dock. If not, Han could watch the Hatteras and try to identify who the owner was. One way or another, he intended to find out more about the emulsion device. In the meantime, though, he had preparations to attend to. He signaled the server to bring his check. Tomorrow was going to be busy, and he needed plenty of rest tonight.

FRIDAY, *mid-morning...*

Baloney was pushing a cart loaded with three heavy five-gallon pails of oil and five boxes of filters down the dock. He stopped out on the finger pier beside *Oar House*. From this vantage point, he could see Han talking with Eric next to *Providence*. Cottell had apparently been unpacking a crate that was sitting on the dock. He was holding something that looked like a small valve and seemed to be explaining its use to Han.

Baloney frowned at the sight. One free beer wasn't enough to change his opinion of Han, whom he still considered to be a major jerk. It felt like he had some sort of ulterior motive, having jumped from his snarky comments yesterday behind *Oar House* to sending him and Betty a round of drinks an hour later. Yeah, something about the man was way south of Kosher.

Baloney unloaded the cart, taking everything into the salon and staging it all next to the engine room hatch in the deck. This wasn't an easy task for one man since each of the three pails weighed almost forty pounds. Even harder was manhandling each one down the short ladder to the engine room deck, about four feet below. He'd just finished moving the third one when a voice came from above in the salon.

"Hey, Gilligan, let me give you a hand with these." Sandy Morgan was now squatting beside the hatch, holding the first of the five small filter boxes.

"Give me... a hand?" Baloney sputtered, "Where the hell were you ten minutes ago when I was wrestlin' these heavy sumbitches?" He indicated the large pails.

"I just got here. So do you want my help or not? Betty said you were 'puttering around' on this rig, and I figured I'd offer to help you, but if you don't want it..." Sandy looked around and said, "Damn, Baloney, you could 'putter around' this thing for a lifetime and still not make a dent in everything that needs to be done."

"Tell me somethin' I don't already know, ya hack. If Debbie wasn't family, an' I mean *good* family, I wouldn't walk away from this thing; I'd *run*! It's a floatin' nightmare."

"Betty told me about the situation. At the risk of being yelled at again, I'll say the same thing I told you yesterday; Gilligan, you're a good man."

"Yeah, well, you're still a hack." But this time, Baloney said it in a somewhat softer tone.

An hour and a half later, Baloney fired up the engines and the generator again, watching the needles on the oil pressure gauges. He wanted to make sure that the pumps were doing their jobs and hadn't gotten air-locked. All were now up into the lower end of the green zones. Going back down into the engine room, he saw that none of the seals on the new oil filters were leaking. The same couldn't be said for the rest of the engines, which had resumed their earlier slow leaks, this time with cleaner, amber-colored oil. Satisfied, he climbed back up out of the engine room and shut everything down.

"Finally! *Now* can we go get some lunch? I'm starved after all this work," Sandy said.

"Work? What work? All ya did was lift three pails ah used oil outta the hatch. Anybody'd think ya rebuilt both engines if they listened ta you!"

"Yes, well, it was labor, and keeping you company while you

cursed up a blue streak was hard work in itself. But we'll call it even after you buy me lunch."

Replacing the oil filters had proven to be a bigger task than Baloney had bargained for. Whoever had last changed them must have been a gorilla, overtightening each one to the point that it took all of Baloney's might to break them free with a strap wrench. He'd slipped on the last one, losing his balance and hitting his head on the other engine, raising an egg-sized bump.

"I'm buyin' you lunch? For two minutes ah work and an hour ah sittin' on your duff?"

"Do you know anyone else who would have as much patience with you? So, yes, you're buying."

"We'll see about that."

THEIR SERVER WAS ONCE AGAIN Angel, who, of course, already knew their beer preferences.

"Hi, guys! Do you need menus?"

Baloney shook his head. "Hey, Angel, not for me. I'll take a Kalik an' a seacake."

Angel nodded. "So I guess this means you're buying, Sandy?"

"In his dreams, Angel. I'll have a seacake and a Red Stripe."

"Got it. Oh, and I get off at four, Baloney, and I figured I'd get cleaned up and change clothes before I stock the bar. I'll be over a little after five if that works for you?"

Baloney looked confused. "Works for me? What bar?"

"The one I'm putting together for *Oar House*. Steven Cohen hired me to bartend on tonight's cruise."

"*Hired*? Ya mean he's payin' ya?"

"Well, yeah! I don't work for free, you know. So, five o'clock? We leave at six, right?"

"Whatever. Yeah, that'd be fine."

"You don't need to worry; Steven already advanced me the cash for the mixers, ice, and liquor. Told me to get nothing but top-shelf alcohol. He wants to make a good impression on his guests."

Sandy could see Baloney was getting mad, so he jumped in. "Oh, I think he's already made quite an impression on Gilligan here." He smiled broadly.

Angel didn't catch the hint. "Yeah, he's an impressive guy. I was surprised that he was able to hire you to run his boat for a booze cruise, Baloney. I didn't know that you freelanced like this. Maybe if you get more of these gigs, you could keep me in mind as a bartender. I think we'd work well together."

Sandy answered quickly before Baloney could, knowing his friend's next words wouldn't be nice ones, even though they wouldn't be directed at Angel. "You know there's no one else he'd rather work these kinds of gigs with."

"Great! Hey, I'll get this order in and be right back with your beer."

After she walked off, Baloney exploded. "Top-shelf liquor? And the cheap son of a bitch *hired* Angel, but I'm supposed to do this for free? The way my niece put it, he was cash poor after buyin' that scow of his, an' that's why I let her talk me inta doin' this. Top-shelf liquor, my ass!"

"Here comes Angel. Just remember, this isn't her fault, Bill. I don't think she knows what is behind this and that you're not happy about it."

"Yeah, I know. She's a good kid. But I think my niece has been bamboozled by this slimeball." It wasn't lost on him that Sandy had just called him "Bill." This was something that rarely happened and only when he wanted Baloney to pay serious attention to what he was saying.

"Here you go, guys." Angel set their beers on the table and turned to leave.

Baloney stopped her by saying, "Hey Angel, if I ever do another of one ah these gigs, you'll be the first bartender I get 'em ta call."

She smiled broadly before heading back to the service bar.

"Gilligan, I said it before, and I'll say it again, you're a goo…"

Sandy couldn't finish the sentence before Baloney held up his palm, stopping him. "Don't say it; I don't wanna hear it. I'll even pay for the beer if you'll shut up."

"Wow. Deal!"

"Ah course, you'll hafta pick up the rest of the lunch, an' I think I'm gonna be up for havin' dessert, too."

4

CON ARTIST CRUISE

"Hello again, *Captain*." The way Steven Cohen emphasized the word "captain" had an almost condescending tone to it, something not lost on Baloney.

"Hello, yourself, Cohen. I hear you hired a bartender an' stocked up with some top-shelf liquor?"

"Well... yes, I did. It's important to me and my business to make a good impression on the people that will be coming along on this little excursion tonight. Or, I should say, it is important to your niece and me since most of them are customers or potential customers of my business—you know, the business she works for.

"It's quite a feather in her cap to get you to run my boat, you know, since you're apparently so well known. And having things go well means I'll be able to keep her on my payroll." He hesitated, looking Baloney up and down. "Is that what you were planning on wearing tonight? I thought you would be wearing some sort of uniform."

Baloney understood the implied but false threat that Debbie's job depended on them having a smooth trip tonight. It didn't sit well with him. Neither did the crack about a uniform. He didn't understand why this clod felt the need to be such a jackass while trying to get his points across.

"Yeah, this is what I'm gonna wear. What's wrong with it?" He had on khaki pants and a long sleeve fishing guide shirt.

"It looks… very *casual*."

"Yeah, well, doin' this is a casual favor ta my niece." He frowned at Cohen. "And ya asked me ta look this rig over and do what needed ta be done ta make sure it's ready ta go. Another favor. So, I checked everything, especially your engines. The oil in 'em hadn't been changed since Reagan was president." He pulled a receipt from his pocket and thrust it at Cohen. "So I changed it. An' here's the bill for the new oil."

Cohen stared at the receipt. "Who the hell told you to change the oil? I'm not paying for this!"

"What, are you kiddin' me? I'll tell ya this, I wasn't takin' this rig out without changin' it. I kinda want ta leave and come back on two engines; ya know what I mean? What came outta those oil pans was sludge! You're just lucky ya didn't seize a bearing on an engine before tonight. Woulda made for a crappy trip ta lose an engine. That, or have the generator crap out in the middle of th' ride. Killin' the lights an' the A/C would kinda throw a wet rag on things no matter what brand ah liquor ya got." He paused, letting that sink in before continuing in a sarcastic tone, "Don't worry, I threw in the labor ta change it for free 'cause I did it myself. You can thank my niece for that. Because havin' a boatyard or a mechanic do it woulda cost ya twice what that bill's for. So, you're welcome."

Cohen scowled. It wasn't a good look for the barely over thirty-year-old with his prematurely receding hairline. He'd tried to counteract it with hair plugs, but by pulling his hair back into his "man-bun," this only accentuated the plugs' cornrow effect in the front. Even though Baloney was a few inches shorter than he was, he could easily see the first couple of rows of hairy plugs. In fact, it was hard for him to keep his gaze from moving upward as they talked.

"All right, I'll pay you for the oil. But don't do anything else without checking with me first."

"I'm not gonna do anything else, period. When we come back an' tie up, I'm done, an' I'll be gone. But if I were you, I'd change that oil again in ten runnin' hours or so, after it has a chance ta flush out any ah that leftover sludge that might be in there."

"What do you mean, gone? I told Debbie I wanted you to show me how to dock this boat!"

Baloney nodded. "Yeah, I will. On the way back in tonight. Give ya a quick lesson."

"Not while there are people around! These are my customers and friends! I'm not having you show me up in front of them."

What an egotistical jerk, Baloney thought. It was all about putting on a dog and pony show with this guy. He was about to give him a piece of his mind when he spotted Angel walking up the gangway, carrying a folding bar table. A cart loaded with coolers and cardboard cases waited on the dock.

"Hey, Baloney. Oh, and hi, Mr. Cohen."

"Angel." Cohen nodded at her. "You can set up the bar over here." He pointed to an area behind the helm chair. "People will be showing up in a half hour, so you need to get ready right away. Captain, go and give her a hand." He walked away from them toward the stern.

Angel saw the look on Baloney's face and knew he was about to explode. She put a hand on his arm and said in a low voice, "Baloney, I really need this gig to go well so I can afford to get my car out of the repair shop." Her eyes were also silently pleading with him.

Baloney sighed, then nodded. "C'mon kid, I'll give ya a hand carryin' th' rest of yer stuff up from the dock."

AFTER HANDLING the dock lines as they cast off, Betty had come over to stand next to Baloney. She watched as he maneuvered *Oar House* away from its slip and then out through the marina basin's inlet. Cohen had been too busy strutting around in front of his guests to take the time to learn. You would have thought he was showing off a brand-new mega yacht instead of an aging Chris Craft.

Betty continued watching Baloney as he navigated their way along the coast of the barrier islands. She'd seen he was in a foul mood as soon as she arrived and had been doing her best to keep him calm since then. It wasn't an easy task since it was obvious that he despised Cohen. It hadn't helped matters when the man spotted Baloney getting ready to light his cigar after they had cleared the breakwater, telling him that cigar smoking wasn't allowed on his boat. This, despite the numerous guests vaping and smoking cigarettes.

Baloney said, "Ya know, if it wasn't for Debbie…"

"But it *is* for Debbie, Bill. Just a couple of hours more, and you'll be finished. Look at it this way; we're getting to see a beautiful sunset together over the barrier islands."

Betty pointed over toward the west, where the sun was barely still above the scrub-covered shore. It was the beginning of what promised to be a beautiful evening. As expected, the ocean was flat-calm, reflecting the sinking orange ball like a huge mirror. There was no other boat traffic in sight, not even any fishermen getting in one last cast of the day. There was only a work barge ahead, anchored a couple of hundred yards offshore.

"We need to do this more often, Bill, on our own boat. I mean, come out and enjoy the sunset. It's like a celebration of the day."

Baloney grunted, "Okay, we will, but just th' two of us. I'm not dragging a buncha yuppies along with us like tonight."

Not only was he not a fan of Cohen's, but he'd realized that most, if not all, of the almost two dozen guests onboard were Cohen's friends. Most were as pompous as he was. Cohen had only told Debbie there were going to be prospective customers along so that she'd talk Baloney into helping her. And then she'd been put to work hauling drinks and appetizers, treated more like a waitress than an associate at his advertising and marketing firm. Not that there was anything wrong with being a server, but it wasn't in the job description when she'd put in her application at Cohen's firm. And it wasn't what her parents had in mind when they scrimped and saved to be able to afford to pay for her college.

HALF AN HOUR LATER, Baloney turned *Oar House* around, starting their roughly hour-long cruise back to *Mallard Cove*. The sun had long since set, and the moon had yet to rise. This post-sunset night was very dark, with only the stars offering any light. Though as far away from any manmade light pollution as they were, the twinkling heavens were indeed spectacular. Unfortunately, only a few of the passengers noticed; most were too busy talking or flirting with each other.

Another consequence of there being no settlements on the barrier islands and with the lights from the few small Eastern Shore towns also being beyond their sight, it was next to impossible to discern the shoreline. Without a working radar, Baloney had only the boat's compass and a GPS-based navigation app on his phone to be able to steer their course by. Which was still enough for him to keep the boat and all its occupants safe but still far less input than he would have liked to have had.

Speaking of their occupants, all that free-flowing booze was having a big effect on them. Voices were getting louder, laughter became more frequent, and folks were less steady on their feet. The only four on the boat who weren't drinking were Debbie, Angel, Baloney, and Betty.

Baloney said, "Betty, would ya go keep an eye on those kids up on the bow? We lose one over th' side on them narrow side decks, an' I couldn't see 'em from here. We'd never know they were missin' 'till we got back ta the dock."

In the daylight, from his position at the helm at the back behind the mid-chest-high raised cabin roof, Baloney had been able to see most of the passengers moving along the side decks and gathering up on the bow. But now, at night, the only lights forward of the helm were some low-mounted deck lights intentionally positioned so as not to interfere with the night vision of whoever was running the boat. Not the greatest situation with a bunch of young, slightly tipsy people moving around that weren't all that familiar with boats in the first place.

"Good idea, hon. I'll go up to the bow, I'll be able to see anybody on the sides since they'll be backlit against the lights in the stern. Do you need anything before I go?"

"Nah, I'm good. Just you be careful."

Cohen now walked up next to Baloney, putting a hand on the stainless-steel steering wheel and crowding him out of the helm seat. "Captain, I'm going to run my boat." He almost slurred the words and looked a bit too impaired to be at the wheel.

"Yeah, I don't think so, Cohen. You've had a few too many."

"I'm not asking your permission, I'm telling you to let go of the wheel!"

"An, I'm tellin' you that you're in no condition ta be runnin' this boat! You'd be puttin' th' lives of everybody aboard in danger. So why don't ya go back ta yer guests an' let me handle it."

"Because it is my boat, and I'll be the one to decide who will run it."

"Yeah, well, I'm the one with the captain's license an' the one that's responsible right now for the safety ah everybody aboard."

"You may have a license, but I do not need one to operate my own boat. Now, let go of that wheel!" He shoved Baloney, trying to get him away from the helm.

"Steven, I thought you were going to let me steer your yacht." A young, very pretty blond woman had walked up, then grabbed Cohen's arm to steady herself. Like Cohen, she looked to be a few drinks past sober.

"I will, Chelsea. But I have to fire my captain first." He turned to Baloney and puffed out his chest, "I'm no longer in need of your services. I want you off my yacht as soon as we reach the dock."

Baloney shook his head as he reluctantly let go of the wheel and moved aside. "Fine, here ya go. I can't stop ya since you own it. But know this; three people I care for are on this rig, an' if anything happens ta any of 'em, I'm gonna hold you responsible. Just for the record, I'm just sayin', neither of ya got any business takin' the wheel right now, an' here in Virginia, ya do need a license."

Baloney turned and made his way up to the bow. Betty and one young couple were the only people there now. The couple was sitting together on the bench seat that was built into the front of the raised cabin top.

Betty was surprised to see her husband. "Bill! What are you doing up here? Why aren't you at the helm?"

"Because that jackass 'fired' me, even though he never hired me inna first place. Tol' me he wanted ta run his own boat."

The young couple, on hearing the conversation, were uncomfortable overhearing their friend referred to as a "jackass." They stood, and in the dim glow from the deck lights, Baloney could barely see the disapproving looks they shot his way before they took their drinks and headed aft.

Betty was understandably concerned about Baloney being removed from the helm. "Can he do that? Is he capable of running the boat?"

"Not even if he was sober, which he ain't. Worse, he's got some little bed-bunny he's gonna let steer. An', yeah, he can do that. Since I wasn't gettin' paid, legally, this ain't a charter. If it was, I'd be responsible for alla th' people onboard 'til we get back ta the dock. But it's his boat, an' he can run it or let whoever he wants to steer it. No matter how dumb an idea that is."

The words were no sooner out of his mouth than the boat lunged forward as someone got into the throttles hard. Baloney had been cruising at a fast idle, with the boat still in displacement mode, parting the water around the bow instead of riding on top of it. Now the aging hull's bow was beginning to rise at an upward angle as it transitioned into planing mode.

Baloney shook his head. "Oh, crap, what a dumbass. He can't see where he's goin' an' can't even tell where th' shore is. I had ta use an app on my phone. Jeeze, he's goin' full throttle now! Let's sit down on that seat before they start ta zig-zaggin' or somethin', an' we end up goin' overboard."

He'd no sooner said that when the boat heeled over as whoever was at the wheel turned hard to starboard, aiming them straight at the shore. Fortunately, they soon turned back out to sea, though not as far as their original course had been taking them.

"Bill, we've got to do something!"

"Nothin' we can do, legally. It's that boy's boat, an' he can do what he wants. I'm pretty sure he's over the legal limit, but I don't know how far. So I couldn't swear ta it in court. Might not make a difference, though, 'cause if he keeps th' throttles firewalled, he's likely ta blow an engine. Those things are old an' run out, an' need ta be babied if he wants 'em ta last much longer."

A chant of "Faster, Chelsea, faster" now broke out among the passengers, who apparently had gathered around the pair back at the helm.

"Faster, hah. There ain't any more speed left in this ol' pig. At least we ain't aimin' for the beach anymore."

Baloney had no sooner said that before twin flashlight beams appeared in the darkness two hundred yards ahead of them, each swinging back and forth. Suddenly Baloney realized they were located about where he had seen that anchored barge earlier. The boat was now headed straight toward the source of the lights. Apparently, these were the only lights on the dark vessel.

Baloney leaped to his feet, yelling, "Turn ta port! Turn ta port!" But whoever was at the helm either didn't hear or understand or maybe chose to ignore him. He raced back along the side deck, intending to turn the wheel himself, but many of the passengers had crowded around Chelsea, who was still at the wheel. Seeing there was no way to get through all the people between himself and the wheel in time, he shouted, "Turn left, damn it, turn left!"

A few of the passengers turned toward him with blank or questioning looks just as the bow of *Oar House* impacted the steel barge with a glancing blow and a sickening crunch of splintering wood. Baloney almost lost his footing, and many others did. He stepped over a few of those who fell as he shoved Chelsea and Cohen out of the way, taking back the helm and bringing the engines down to idle. He spun the wheel, slowly bringing the boat back around and heading back to the barge.

"What did we hit?" Cohen asked.

"A barge. They're supposed ta have an anchor light, but this one didn't. There were some people on board with flashlights, waving ya off. That's why I was yellin' for ya ta turn."

"I didn't hear you yell anything. And why are you going back?"

"We need ta find out if anybody on it got hurt. Meantime, ya need ta check on alla yer friends, too. Make sure none ah them went overboard or got hurt, either."

"Screw those people on the barge. Though I should sue their asses."

"Will ya go and check on yer friends!" He glared at Cohen until he started helping some people up off the deck.

"Bill, are you okay?" Betty had just reached the helm after racing back from the bow.

"Yeah, no thanks ta th' whiz kid over there. You hurt?"

"No. Thank goodness you had us sit down on that bench. The noise up there, when we hit, was awful."

"Yeah, you wanna go down below an' check th' bow for damage? See if we're takin' on any water. I'd go, but I gotta check on the barge we hit. Check on Debbie while yer at it, too."

"Right." She disappeared below.

Baloney looked around behind his helm seat to where the bar had been. The table was still upright, but most of the bottles were on the deck, and many had broken. Angel was busy salvaging what she could and picking up the larger pieces of jagged glass.

"You all right, Angel?"

"Yeah, Baloney, I fell against that girl who was steering, and it saved me from going all the way down and hitting the deck." She paused a few beats before adding, "You tried to warn them."

"Yeah, well, that ship has sailed already. Now we gotta check an' see if they hurt anybody else." He looked around at the passengers, who didn't seem to be seriously hurt, with the exception of numerous bumps and bruises. "Looks like we all got lucky. Now we gotta see if th' folks on that barge did, too."

Baloney looked at the labels below the switches next to the helm until he found the one he wanted. Flipping the switch, he was relieved to find the forward docking lights attached to the top of the wheelhouse still worked. As the light began to illuminate the barge, he saw two men using flashlights while staring down at the side of the barge's hull. A large white blaze marked the point of impact.

As Baloney turned *Oar House,* preparing to pull up alongside the barge, the docking light swept across more of its deck. He got a brief glimpse of pieces of machinery and what had apparently been large wooden crates, along with a weird-looking thing that appeared to be a leather stingray. As the lights continued across the deck, at one end, a shipping container sat with its doors open, its interior mostly shaded in darkness. He also got a brief glimpse of the outline of a large boat as it receded into the darkness beyond the barge and out of range of *Oar House*'s lights. It had apparently been either tied up on the far side of the barge or possibly had already been pulling away when the collision occurred. The glimpse he got of it reminded him of something he'd seen before, but it didn't quite register.

One of the two men on the barge was now screaming at Baloney, "You hit my boat! You pay me!" He had a heavy Asian accent, but Baloney could barely see them in the dim spill from the cabin lights since the docking lights were now faced out in the water.

"Yer nuts! Ya don't even have an anchor light. You should pay me! An' it's a friggin' barge, not a boat, ya dumbass!"

The other man grabbed the arm of the one who was shouting and said something to him quietly. Then the first man yelled, "I no pay you, you drive crazy."

Cohen was now standing next to Baloney. "We need to get their information because I'm going to sue them for the damage to my boat!"

Baloney leaned in toward Cohen and said quietly, "No, yer not. Because if ya did, that would mean callin' the Coast Guard out here right now ta make a report. An they'd want a blood sample from you and yer pal Chelsea, and I'm guessin' ya don't want that ta happen. Unless ya want both of ya ta go ta jail fer operatin' a vessel under th' influence. They've been gettin' real strict on that lately."

"Then we can just say that you were at the helm."

"No, we can't. And no, we're not going to." Debbie had come up beside Baloney and was glaring at her boss. "That would affect my uncle's captain's license, which he needs for his business. You wanted to do this to him after he was doing this as a favor for me? You've done nothing but treat him and me badly from the minute we stepped aboard this boat."

"And you have apparently forgotten that you need your job, which you are about to lose," Cohen replied angrily.

"No, I haven't, and I'm not about to lose it because I already quit." She turned to Baloney. "Uncle Bill; I'm sorry I got you involved in this."

Baloney smiled at her. "Ya know, I'm not sorry. Seein' ya stand up ta this jackass was worth all the trouble, kiddo."

Betty came up from the cabin. "Well, the hull's got a couple of cracked ribs and probably a split bow stem. But at least the damage is above the waterline, and I didn't see anything seeping into the bilge. I wouldn't push her hard, but we should be okay to cruise back slowly."

"In that case, I'll run us back, so we can make sure ta get home in one piece. Angel, pack up th' bar; it's past last call."

"Who the hell do you think you are? This is my boat, and I'll decide when the bar gets closed," Cohen yelled at Baloney.

Baloney picked up the microphone from the VHF radio as he stared at Cohen. "Oh yeah? Well, then maybe we should give 'em a call an' let th' Coasties decide."

"C'mon, baby, let's just go down into the cabin." Chelsea tugged at Cohen's arm, urging him toward the hatchway. The collision had sobered her up slightly, enough to realize she didn't want anything to do with the Coast Guard.

Cohen hissed, "I still want you off my boat as soon as we hit the dock, Cooper."

"Well, Junior, since I'm runnin' the boat, we won't be hittin' the dock; we'll be tyin' up nice an' easy. An' ya don't hafta worry about me gettin' off when we do 'cause I can't wait. An' speakin' about not waitin', ya need ta settle up with Angel here right now, so we don't hafta hunt ya down when we get back. An' if I were you, I'd make sure ta tip her real good so she forgets all about what happened tonight. Not reportin' a boating accident is real serious business, ya know."

The accident had turned the festive mood more somber as it sunk into some of the passengers about how lucky they were and how much more serious the accident could have been. They all now avoided the helm area, wanting to stay clear of "Captain Buzz-Kill," as one of them had nicknamed Baloney.

Debbie was still standing next to Baloney. "I'm going to go clear out my desk tomorrow and start looking for another job. I am so, so sorry I got you involved in this, Uncle Bill. I should've realized what Steven was really like, but I couldn't see past trying to save my job."

"Yeah, a job's an important thing, kiddo. When we were startin' our charter business, I put up with more than our share of jerks. I was so scared ah one of 'em talkin' bad about us. But ya know what I finally figured out? The only people that'd listen ta a jerk are other jerks. An' that's not who we wanted as charters.

"So, I started tellin' things like they were, an' if people didn't like that, I didn't like them. Ya learned a lesson tonight that most folks take a lot longer ta figure out. Life's not just about a job. Don't get me wrong, ya need one ah those so ya can eat, but it ain't everything. Ya want one where you're around people that are good people, not jerks. There's always some jackass around; ya can't avoid alla them, but ya need ta find a place that's got good people. A place where you'll be appreciated. Which is why tomorra I'm gonna call *Tuna Hunters Productions* an put in a good word for ya. They're adding some new shows, an' their publicity department is swamped. I'm thinkin' you'd be a good fit. It never hurts ta ask."

Debbie hugged her uncle, not just because he was going to make that call but because it meant he didn't hold tonight's events against her. When she released him, she saw he was smiling. Then he pulled a fresh cigar out of his shirt pocket. As he lit it, the smile got wider.

"Another important thing ta learn, kiddo, is ya gotta live life on yer own terms. Ya need ta steer clear ah anybody who tries changin' that." He took a long draw from the stogie and then let out a very satisfying puff of smoke.

THE LIGHT OF DAY

S*aturday, shortly after 7:00 a.m....*

"I NEED to get to the hospital to check on my friend. Can't we do this later?" Sandy asked the Northampton County Sheriff's Department detective who was interviewing him. He was sitting on a bench on the walkway behind *My Mahi*. The boat was swarming with crime scene techs and the coroner, who had yet to remove Betty Cooper's body. The dock behind charter boat row was cordoned off with yellow plastic crime scene tape. The whole scene seemed so surreal.

"No, we can't. Last I heard, your friend was in surgery and will be for quite a while, so there's no rush for you to get over there. Now back to what I was asking you. This is the cat you said led you to the victims?" He pointed to KC, who had curled beside Sandy on the bench.

"No, it was the Cheshire Cat from *Alice in Wonderland. Of course,* this is the cat. Do you see any others around here? But what difference does it make? It isn't like you can question him, too! Look, if you want to keep asking me dumb questions, you can do that at the hospital."

The detective snapped back, "What's dumb is expecting me to believe that out of the blue, your cat wakes you up and leads you over here in the dark like some kind of feline 'Lassie.' You'll either cooperate with me here, or I'll take you into custody as a material witness, and then we'll go to the Sheriff's Office."

A deputy approached the pair and motioned for the detective to come over to where he was standing. It was apparent that the detective was unhappy about being pulled away from Sandy, but he walked over and conferred with the deputy in hushed tones. When he returned, Sandy noted a change in his demeanor, now even more direct and forceful.

"Do you know of a boat called the *Oar House*, Mr. Morgan?"

Sandy replied, "Yeah, it's one that Baloney, er, Captain Cooper, ran on a booze cruise last night. It belongs to his niece's boss, who just bought it. Bill ran the trip as a favor to her because the guy doesn't know how to run it yet. Why?"

"Were you aboard it this morning?"

"What? No. The only time I've even been near it was to help Captain Cooper change the oil before he took it on last night's run. I don't even know the owner.

"Like I told you, when he woke me up, I followed KC straight here to find out what was bugging him. After I discovered Bill and Betty, I went up to the restaurant to get help. I went back to Bill, trying to keep pressure on the open wounds to keep him from bleeding out before EMS could arrive.

"I don't make a habit of boarding strangers' boats in the middle of the night, and I had no reason to be around *Oar House*. What's that got to do with Betty and Bill?"

"There was a blood trail leading to *My Mahi* from there. We just discovered two more bodies aboard it; both of them had been stabbed as well."

Sandy was visibly startled at the news of more victims. "So

whoever killed those people came over here and attacked Betty and Bill?"

"Probably. And you have a connection to both boats. I think you and I need to continue this conversation down at the Sheriff's Office."

Sandy didn't like where the detective was apparently heading with his questions. "No, I'm staying right here, and I think I'm done talking for now. One of my friends is dead, I don't even know for sure that the other is still alive, and now I find out there are two more murders. Instead of trying to find their killer or killers, all you want to do is threaten me and talk about my cat. This, and infer that I had been aboard that boat where those other people were attacked. No, I'm not saying anything else without a lawyer."

"Hold on; you're not under arrest. Yet."

"Un huh, 'yet.' That's what I'm talking about and why I want a lawyer here to defend my rights. Here's the thing, I found my friends, and I went for help. Period. I never went near that other boat today, and you're wasting your time questioning me. There's nothing more that I can tell you."

"We're just talking here, so you don't need a lawyer. But according to several people, you are known for getting into frequent arguments with Captain Cooper in the bars here."

"Oh, for Pete's sake, that's what we *do*! We argue over who is going to pay for the beer we drink. We've done that from the very first day I met him a couple of years ago." Sandy shook his head.

"So, he owed you money?"

"What? No! It's a running gag between the two of us. Neither of us is hurting for money." He pointed at the two Dolphin Fleet boats. "Bill and Betty don't owe a dime on either of those rigs or the one he's rebuilding over at *Albury's*. He makes a ton of money on that cable fishing show."

"So you're jealous of that."

"What? No! I make a hell of a lot more than he does from my books and the movies that have been made from them, so no, there's nothing for me to be jealous of."

"Maybe you were jealous of his wife..."

Sandy was up off the bench in an instant, putting his face within inches of the detective's. "You watch your damn mouth! Betty was my friend, and there was no couple ever more suited for each other or dedicated to one another…"

"You're headed in the wrong direction, Officer." Michael "Murph" Murphy had appeared at the railing of the restaurant's elevated deck behind the two of them. He was holding a smartphone that was playing a security camera video.

The detective snapped, "That's Detective Aldrich, not 'officer.' I'm conducting an investigation here, and that deck is closed. So you can't be there; you need to go back inside the restaurant."

"I'm Michael Murphy, and I own *Mallard Cove*. This deck isn't part of your crime scene, but it is my property, so I'll stand here if I want. And I believe I overheard my friend say that he wanted a lawyer to be present. I'll be glad to put in a call for my attorney Howard Falcon, and we can wait until he gets here if you want to continue." He held up the phone. "Or, you can clear him right now. This is a video of the security camera feed from over at the gate by the boat barn that leads to our private marina where Sandy lives. You'll see KC walking in this direction about a quarter to five this morning and running back ten minutes later. Then he and Sandy come back through the gate at five. The video is time-stamped and covers the last twenty-four hours."

Murph held it out, and Aldrich frowned as he reached up and grabbed it. "Why do you have a criminal defense attorney, Murphy?"

"Because of the Northampton County Sheriff's Office. I met Howard when he intervened on behalf of my partner, Casey Shaw, who was being falsely accused at the time by people in your office. You've probably heard about that; it didn't end well for the last Commonwealth Attorney and a few folks you used to work with, including that last sheriff." He waited for a beat to let that part sink in. Howard Falcon was the best and most well-known defense attorney in Virginia. "Bill and Betty are my friends, just as Sandy is. And I'm telling you that you're wasting time looking at him."

"I'll be the judge of that." He looked at the video and then at Sandy, who had sat back down on the bench. He then handed the phone back to Murph. "Forward that video to my office. Here's my card with my email address." He turned back to Sandy. "If I have any more questions after I review the video more closely, I'll be in touch with you, Morgan. So, don't leave the area."

"Don't worry about me; you just find out who attacked my friends —it wasn't me."

"Like I said, I'll be the judge of that. Now you need to get away from my crime scene." The detective pointed out toward the parking lot beyond the yellow tape.

KC followed Sandy as he ducked under the tape. Murph met the two in the parking lot, which was now filled with both marked and unmarked law enforcement vehicles as well as the coroner's van.

A clearly shaken Sandy said, "Thanks for standing up for me, Murph. Northampton SO is doing an incompetent job of investigating again, as usual." He paused a few seconds and seemed to get some of his composure back. "Has anyone told Casey, Dawn, Marlin, and Kari yet?"

Marlin Denton was the head of the foundation that owned *Tuna Hunters*, and his wife Kari was in charge of Shaw Properties' management and acquisitions group. Both lived aboard their large house barge in *Casey's Cove* and were close friends of Baloney and Betty's.

Murph nodded. "Lindsay was calling everybody as I left to come over here after Mimi called us. Linds was also calling Rikki."

Rikki Jenkins was another friend of Baloney and Betty's and owned ESVA Security, a national private security company that had strong connections with a lot of government groups. They were the "go-to" organization for when the US government had a mess within its borders but needed to make sure there was nothing about the cleanup that could point back to any department. ESVA Security's unofficial motto was: "Plausible deniability... for a price." And it was usually a very big price.

Sandy nodded. "Good thinking. We could use her here."

"Yeah, especially since it first looked like that idiot detective was trying to pin this on you when I got here." The group of friends they are part of, known as *Casey's Crew*, have had had a couple of run-ins with the Sheriff's Office of Northampton County. None of these had left them with anything approaching an impression of competency. The most recent one had raised serious questions about possible corruption that reached all the way to the top of the department.

Sandy looked up as a young woman came rushing through the maze of vehicles with a confused and worried look on her face. She spotted Sandy and hurried toward him. They'd met a couple of times since she'd moved to the area. Sandy said to Murph, "Aw, damn, it's Debbie, their niece."

"Hey, Mr. Morgan, what's going on here?" That's when she spotted the yellow tape and saw the techs and deputies in the cockpit of *My Mahi*. "Oh, my God! Aunt Betty, Uncle Bill! Are they all right? What's happened?"

She no sooner got the words out than the coroner and an assistant began bringing Betty's body out of the cabin in a black bag.

Sandy reached out and grabbed Debbie's upper arms, trying to draw her attention away from the scene on *My Mahi*. "Debbie, Bill and Betty were attacked last night on their boat. Bill is in surgery, but I'm sorry, your aunt is gone."

At first, her face registered total shock, which quickly switched to anguish as she let out a scream. "Noooooo..." Her knees buckled, and if Sandy hadn't had hold of her upper arms, she would've collapsed. The scream became more of a wail, and then as Sandy wrapped his arms around her and gathered her in close, the wail turned into sobs.

"Aunt... Betty... can't... be gone. She can't..."

Sandy patted her back softly, saying, "I know, I know. I'm so sorry." He held her for several minutes as he and Murph stood in the parking lot with her until her sobs began to subside. "There's nothing that we can do here, Debbie. Let me drive you to the hospital so at least we can be there for your uncle when he gets out of surgery."

Debbie nodded and allowed herself to be led over to *Casey's Cove* with Sandy and Murph. Once there, Murph went home to see whom Lindsay had managed to reach, while Sandy and Debbie got into his truck, then headed to the hospital.

This early on a Saturday, the emergency room shouldn't have had a chance to get busy yet; at least, that was what Sandy was hoping. The nurse at the desk said that Baloney had been taken straight into surgery and directed them to another nurse next to the surgical waiting area down a long hall.

After confirming that Debbie was his next of kin, that nurse said Baloney was indeed alive and still in surgery. She added that he would probably be in there for quite a bit longer as his wounds were quite extensive. They wouldn't know anything for a while. Then Debbie and Sandy settled in on a couch near the door in the waiting room.

"I don't understand, Mr. Morgan; everybody loves my aunt and uncle. Who would want to do something like this?"

"I don't know, Debbie. And why would they want to harm those people on *Oar House*?"

"What are you talking about?"

"The two people who were murdered there." He saw the shock register on her face again. It suddenly dawned on him that she hadn't gotten there until after Aldrich had told him and Murph about the additional two victims being discovered.

"Which ones... do you know who they were?"

"The detective only told me that two people were killed; he didn't give me any details other than the attack on your aunt and uncle was connected to the one on *Oar House*."

Their conversation was interrupted as Marlin and Kari Denton arrived, along with Murph and Lindsay. Marlin asked Sandy, "How's Bill?"

"Still in surgery, and it could be a while."

Marlin grimaced, then realized that Debbie was there. "Are you Debbie?" When she nodded, he introduced himself and the others. "Your uncle is an old friend and the reason I first came to live at *Mallard Cove*. And your aunt... I'm so sorry. Such a sweet person and a good friend."

Debbie nodded, not saying anything while she wiped away tears. Lindsay sat down beside her and put an arm around her shoulders. An awkward silence fell over the room. Though they'd all heard about Debbie, only Sandy had met her before. And while they all felt a profound sense of loss for their friend Betty, none of theirs was a familial loss like Debbie's.

Suddenly Debbie realized that she hadn't called to let her parents know what had happened. She excused herself as she got up to go outside to make the call that she was now dreading.

After she left the room, Sandy asked Murph, "Any idea who the other two victims were?"

Murph looked taken aback, "What other victims?"

Sandy replied, "Aldrich must've told me before you came over to talk to him. They found two more people stabbed to death aboard *Oar House,* the Chris Craft that Baloney ran last night. They found a trail of blood drops that led from there over to *My Mahi,* so those two were attacked before Betty and Bill." It hit him that he'd called Baloney "Bill" again, like he was unconsciously distancing himself in case the worst-case scenario came to be. He made a mental note not to do that again.

Murph and Lindsay now glanced worriedly at each other. They'd lost one good friend and were in danger of losing another. In addition to this, the business that they were the majority owners of was now going to become infamous for multiple, as yet unsolved, murders. Not something that you wanted your marina, hotel, restaurants, and bars to be connected with.

Murph said, "I hadn't heard about the attacks on *Oar House.* The parking lot was so jammed with cop cars that we didn't get near that other dock and had no way of knowing." He sighed. While the effect this would have on their business was one thing they had to worry about, losing Betty was absolutely devastating to Lindsay and him. And now, the uncertainty of Baloney's condition was agonizing. Having him pull through was their primary focus and concern. He and Lindsay could deal with the business part of things later.

Rikki Jenkins and her partner Cindy Crenshaw now arrived at the waiting room. The two lived aboard their older Hatteras Motoryacht *Hibiscus* at the *Bayside Resort and Marina* on the Eastern Shore. This property was also owned by the Shaw's investment group, which they were both also involved in.

Cindy, a shapely woman in her mid-thirties with curly shoulder-length hair, managed all of the *Bayside* businesses and properties. Rikki was a few years younger and an inch taller and had been described as having a "severe beauty" as compared to Cindy's softer features. Rikki had short, platinum-blond hair and ice-blue eyes that you could see from across most rooms. The combination was stunning.

Of the two, Cindy was the one who you would want to comfort you in a crisis, while Rikki was who you would want to take control of the situation. In this case, the timing of their arrival was perfect. Things were going to get busy in the waiting room as word of what happened began to spread. Sandy brought the two up to date with everything they knew so far.

Marlin finished reading a text on his phone, then looked up. "B2 said the word is getting out among the charter boat crews, and they are asking him for news and want to know what they can do to help." B2 was the nickname of Bobby Smith, the young man who used to be Baloney's mate before he got promoted to captain of the *Golden Dolphin* after Baloney bought *My Mahi*. "He still took his own charter out, figuring that's what Baloney would want him to do."

"And Baloney would have had his ass if he had canceled on his people," Sandy said. This brought a small chuckle from the group, knowing this was true. It was also a much-needed bit of relief from the tension they were all feeling, and it was somehow reassuring. It almost felt as if Baloney was issuing telepathic orders from the operating table.

"Tell him that we're still waiting on news from the doctors and that Baloney can use all their prayers now. Put it out over the VHF so that everybody on the boats gets it at once, and we'll text him when we know more."

The local charter boat community used VHF radios to communicate when they wanted the other boats to hear them. Though secret hot spots were usually only shared by cell phone with other cooperating boats and crews. The running joke was that Baloney was so loud he wasted his money buying a VHF since they were only good for "line of sight," and if you could see him, you could hear him, no matter the distance.

Debbie came back in and said she'd managed to talk her mother out of driving down right away, at least until they knew more about Bill. She told her there was nothing they could do about her sister, and now all they could do about Bill was wait.

Debbie's earlier hysterics had completely disappeared, replaced now by a tough and logical determination not often found in someone in their early twenties. It was like she'd aged ten years since she'd left the room and returned. Then again, they all felt much older now than they had when they'd awakened today. They all began to settle in now for what they knew would be a long day.

HE SAW the blocked number and wasn't surprised since it was on his burner phone's screen.

"Yeah?"

"One of my men was… careless this morning and left something behind. Something that could cause problems if it became linked to me."

"What is it?"

"Something he left in Cooper at *Mallard Cove*. You can figure it out; that is why I pay you. That, and to take care of problems. If that item gets logged in as evidence, I am not the only one who will have problems."

There was a few seconds of silence before he answered, "I got it. An' I know what you're talkin' about. I'll handle it." There were several seconds of silence before he realized the caller had already hung up.

6

THE WAITING GAME

S*aturday, 9:30 a.m.*

Detective Aldrich walked into the hospital on a two-pronged mission. First, he needed to retrieve the knife that had been left in Cooper's chest. Second, he wanted to find Cooper's niece, who he'd learned was aboard *Oar House* the previous night. He figured she would be here, waiting for news on her uncle, and he had several questions to ask her.

At the nurse's desk, Aldrich was told to wait in the surgery area while someone went to retrieve the knife. That nurse returned with the knife in a small stainless-steel tray where the surgeon had placed it after she had removed it from Baloney's chest. The handle and blade were covered in now-drying blood. Aldrich used a glove to pick it up and transfer it to a clear plastic evidence bag.

Aldrich walked into the surgery waiting room, spotting Murphy and Morgan in a group of several people. Sitting next to Morgan was a young dark-haired woman with a very sad and concerned look on her face. He walked up to her, ignoring Morgan's glare.

"Miss Ramsey?"

The woman looked up. "Yes?" Then, she saw the knife in the plastic bag he was holding, and she went from looking concerned to being horrified and scared.

Realizing his mistake, Aldrich turned away, out of her direct vision, as he wrapped the excess plastic of the bag around the knife, obscuring its view. But this was not before Rikki, who was standing right next to him, managed to get a good look at it. He then shoved it in his waistband in the small of his back as he turned back toward Debbie.

"I apologize; I didn't mean to upset you. Are you Miss Ramsey?"

"Yes?"

"I'm Detective Aldrich, and I'm investigating last night's attacks on your uncle and aunt and the two people on the Chris Craft that's called the *Oar House*."

"Who were the two on that boat who were killed?"

"We're not releasing their names until we notify their next of kin."

She nodded, then said, "I wasn't around when any of this happened, you know."

"I understand that. But the bartender that was on the trip said there was an incident aboard when you were. Actually, a few separate incidents. Can you tell me what happened?"

She sighed, realizing that these were the final memories she would ever have of her Aunt Betty and possibly the last she'd have of her Uncle Bill.

"I had talked my uncle into running my now ex-boss's boat on an evening cruise..."

Aldrich interrupted. "You said 'ex-boss'?"

"Yeah, he was being a jerk, so I ended up quitting last night when we were out on the boat."

"What, was he hitting on you or harassing you?"

"No, nothing like that. He was giving my uncle a hard time, even though he was doing him a favor. Anyway, my boss, Steven Cohen, had a few drinks and demanded to run the boat, even though he didn't know what he was doing. Uncle Bill told him that wasn't a good idea, but Steven got mad and told him he was fired, even though he wasn't technically working for him and wasn't even getting paid.

"Then Uncle Bill went up on the bow to be with Aunt Betty, and Steven let this girl Chelsea take the wheel. She knew even less than Steven and went full speed, turning back and forth. A couple of minutes later, she hit a barge, bouncing off the side. Uncle Bill came running back and took over, slowing us down and turning around to go back to check on the barge. The two Asian-sounding guys that were on it were really mad and told Uncle Bill to pay them, even though they didn't have any real damage, and there hadn't been any anchor lights on their barge.

"Steven was just as mad and wanted them to pay for the damage to his boat. But Uncle Bill told him that taking them to court meant he'd have to make a report with the Coast Guard right then, who would probably want to check Steven and Chelsea for alcohol. Then Steven suggested they could just say that Uncle Bill had been the one who hit the barge. I told him that he could forget it; he wasn't going to blame Uncle Bill for something he didn't do. That was it for me; I'd had enough and quit right there."

"So, it's safe to say that your uncle and Steven Cohen were mad at each other?"

"More like Uncle Bill was disgusted, and Steven was the angry one."

"Angry enough to hit him?"

Debbie didn't hesitate. "No way. Steven is more like a showboat than a fighter. After Uncle Bill took over, he and Chelsea went down to his bedroom, and I never saw them again before I got off the boat back at the dock."

"Could someone have been hiding in his room when they went in?"

"Maybe, I guess so; why? Wait, were they the ones that were killed?"

"Again, I can't comment on who the victims were. Did your uncle get off the boat with you?"

"Yeah, he and my aunt did after we all helped the bartender,

Angel, finish cleaning up. We only did that so she could get out of there faster, then all four of us left together."

"So, he and Steven Cohen never saw each other again last night, as far as you know?"

"Right, and that's all I know. Now if you don't mind, I just want to be left alone."

Aldrich started to say something but thought better of it and nodded. He took a card out of his pocket and handed it to her. "If you think of anything else, please give me a call. Even if it's just some small detail that seems out of place or sticks out in your mind. Sometimes these things can take a little time to remember. And if you can, give me a number where I can reach you." He handed her a small notepad and a pen, and she jotted down her cell phone number.

As Aldrich was leaving, Rikki followed him out into the hallway.

"Hi, Detective; I'm Rikki Jenkins of ESVA Security."

Aldrich stopped and turned to her. "I've heard of your company. What can I do for you?"

"I couldn't help but notice that knife you have. I'm guessing that it was the one used to attack Bill Cooper?"

"I'm not going to comment on an ongoing investigation."

"Right. But you saw that it's a QNL-95, right? That's the same model the Chinese Armed Forces carry."

"So, what's your point? Everything is made in China these days."

"Debbie said the men on the barge sounded Asian."

"So does everyone who works at the Chinese restaurants on the Shore, but that doesn't make them all suspects. Look, lady, leave the investigation to the professionals. If we need to find out if someone's spouse is cheating on them, we'll be sure to give your outfit a call." He turned and left.

Rikki was angry but not surprised. Things at the Northampton Sheriff's Department had not gotten better with the arrival of Sheriff Bromwell. This Aldrich guy was typical of the high level of arrogance and ignorance among their new hires. He'd probably missed the fact that this particular knife had bayonet mounts. It was an actual

Chinese Armed Forces bayonet that was standard issue for them, not some knockoff you could buy online.

While she didn't want to jump to conclusions, Baloney getting into an argument with two Asian men who blamed him for colliding with their barge just hours before he was attacked with a Chinese military knife was quite a coincidence. Not that Rikki believed in those. And all four victims were apparently aboard the boat that collided with the barge—another coincidence. But if there wasn't any damage, why would one or both of them come after Baloney, and why kill the people on the *Oar House*? How would they know where to find them? None of this made any sense.

When she returned to the waiting room, Sandy looked up at her. He'd seen her take off after Aldrich and was wondering why. She knew what he was thinking and quickly glanced over at Debbie, then back to him, giving him an almost imperceptible shake of her head. He nodded, understanding that answers might come later, in private.

Casey and Dawn Shaw walked in, both looking as concerned as the rest felt. Dawn said, "Sorry to have taken so long to get here. Everything is taking me longer these days." Dawn was six months pregnant. "Any news?"

Sandy shook his head. "Not yet. Though, at this point, I'm taking that as a positive." He didn't have to say what the rest were thinking: they would've already been told if they'd lost Bill.

Soon after the Shaws arrived, the Reverend Eddie Jones, more commonly known as "Rev," came in. A former waterman who heeded a different calling in midlife, he was also a member of *Casey's Crew* and a good friend of Baloney's. There was something special about the guy. Merely by being there, he seemed to have brought with him a feeling of hopefulness that spread amongst everyone in the room.

Two and a half hours later, a very tired-looking middle-aged woman in surgical scrubs walked in and asked for Baloney's family.

Debbie replied, "I'm his niece, but we're all his family."

"Okay. He's being moved into the Surgical Intensive Care Unit. I'd like to be as positive for you as I can about his prognosis, but the truth is, he has a long way to go before he'll be out of the woods.

"He lost so much blood before he got here; he went into cardiac arrest before we could even start working on him. He'd lost over fifty percent of his blood volume by that point, so his heart had quit trying to pump. We replaced blood as fast as we could and got his heart going again. At that point, we concentrated on getting his blood pressure up, and then we started working on the bleeders.

"Thankfully, no one tried removing that knife before we got him into the operating room. There's no way it could have been done successfully in the field; we were prepared to deal with that bleeding, and it was still a challenge for me and my team.

"While his prognosis is guarded, I can tell you this; he's one tough guy, and he's got that going for him. His heart stopped again while we were working on him, but we were able to defibrillate him a second time and get it going again. I've never had a patient who had been stabbed as many times as he had that even made it into the OR. It would be shorter and easier to tell you what organs weren't damaged than list the ones that were.

"If he survives, you can expect him to be in intensive care for several days. We'll be watching him closely for any signs of infection. With so many wounds and sutures, especially in the intestines, there are a lot of places for infection to start. No matter what, he'll have a long, hard road ahead of him.

"Assuming he makes progress, we'll keep him sedated for a bit since we don't want him moving around before he can begin healing. And that's in addition to what we'll be giving him for pain. So he won't be awake anytime soon; after he is, he'll be foggy for a while. Also, while he's in the intensive care unit, only two family members are allowed to visit for a few minutes at the top of each hour. Right now, I'd advise against that for a day or two. So, why don't you all go home and get some rest."

Debbie said, "I want to stay and see him before I go."

"I do, too," Sandy added.

The doctor looked like she clearly disagreed with the idea but said begrudgingly, "All right, but be prepared; he has a lot of tubes and drains and a machine that's helping him breathe."

EVEN HAVING BEEN TOLD to prepare themselves, Debbie and Sandy still were shocked by what they saw. If they hadn't been told this was Bill Cooper, there's no way they would have recognized him at first glance. Breathing tubes hid part of his face; what part of it they could see had a gray, waxy appearance. While not a large man to begin with, he looked even more slight, gaunt, and more than ten years older, lying in that hospital bed.

With his eyes closed, Baloney looked more dead than alive. Only the constant beep of the machine tracking his heartbeat and the shallow rise and fall of his chest reassured them that he wasn't. The only signs of trauma were bandages on both arms and his left hand, probably covering defensive wounds he got from fighting off his attacker.

Debbie gently took his right hand, and with tears streaming down her face, she said, "Get better, Uncle Bill; I need you."

Sandy leaned close to his ear and said, "Get your ass out of this bed, Gilligan. When you do, the first round is on me."

Neither message seemed to register, not that either of the pair had expected them to. Out in the hall, Rev was waiting for them. "I encouraged everyone else to go home and get some rest. I've been through this before. It isn't going to be a sprint; more like a marathon."

"Thank you. And Mr. Morgan, why did you call him Gilligan?"

"Call me Sandy. If I had called him Bill, he would've thought that I believed he was dying." For the first time today, Sandy managed a slight smile. "He hates it when I call him Gilligan and always has a smart-ass reply. And he never, ever, turns down a free beer."

7

____

SWITCHEROO

"Yeah, I just heard from Rev, and Baloney is in real rough shape. If he makes it, he'll be in the hospital for a good while. An' they don't want anybody but family to visit. He's in intensive care, so no flowers or cards or stuff. He'll be knocked out for at least a couple ah days. That's all I know for now, guys, but I'll keep y'all up to date when I hear anything more. *Golden Dolphin*, out." B2 had been updating the charter crews over the VHF. But they weren't the only ones who tuned in.

~

"So, Bigmouth has survived, after all. This just means it will be more difficult to silence him where he is. Difficult but not impossible, and it must be done before he is able to talk to the police and tell them what he might have seen. At least he cannot talk before tonight's mission. However, it will only be a complete success if they are not able to identify the launch boat. To ensure that, Bigmouth must die very soon..."

He reached for his phone.

~

REV FOLLOWED Sandy back to *Mallard Cove*, where he dropped Debbie at her car. As she left, the two men saw that B2 was pulling in with the *Golden Dolphin*, and they went over to talk with him. They watched as he and his mate unloaded and began cleaning the day's catch, a decent number of Spanish mackerel.

Sandy looked over at the cockpit of *My Mahi* in the next slip. The yellow crime tape had been removed, and there were no seals on the cabin door, but the cockpit was a mess, with dried blood and discarded bandages and wrappers strewn about.

"Give me a hand, Rev."

They stepped into the cockpit, gathering up all the debris left behind by the paramedics. Next, they began washing down the deck, scrubbing and rinsing away all the blood. A couple of tourists on the dock began taking pictures of what they were doing, angering Sandy. He yelled, "Why don't you idiots go take pictures of seagulls or something?"

One of them asked, "Isn't this Captain Baloney's boat from that *Tuna Hunters* show? We heard he was murdered on it this morning."

All the rage that had been subconsciously building in Sandy instantly came to the surface. He yelled again, "*NO, he is NOT dead!* But you might be if you don't get the hell away from here!" With that, he turned the hose on the tourists, soaking and sending them scurrying away as they cursed him. He felt a hand on his shoulder. Rev's.

"It's okay, Sandy."

"No, it's not. You know goddamn well it's not okay, Rev. It may never be okay again." He took in a deep breath.

"Hey, Sandy, you okay?" A very concerned B2 joined them in the cockpit. He'd heard the yelling and seen Sandy soaking the tourists.

Rev saw Sandy struggling to keep from exploding after hearing the word "okay" again. He answered for him. "I don't think any of us are, Bobby. How are you coping?"

B2 hung his head a little, "I kinda lost it up on the flybridge earlier. It was like I was runnin' the boat in a daze. I can't believe that Betty's gone, and I hope and pray Baloney pulls through. They're not just my business partners; they're more like my family."

"Yeah, Bobby, they're like family to all of us." Sandy had now gotten his temper in check as he realized that everyone else was hurting like he was, especially Bobby.

B2 joined them down in the cockpit, helping erase the last traces of blood. Sandy asked, "Don't you need to help your mate?"

"Nah, he's got it. I told him he could have my share of the tips since he's been taking up my slack all day." He looked over at the cabin door. "How bad is the cabin?"

Sandy replied, "Bad. And we're going to have to do something about it next."

Sandy led the two men inside. Blood and signs of the struggle were everywhere. This was apparently where most of the fight between Baloney and his assailant must have happened. They followed the blood trail down the stairs and into the master stateroom to the blood-soaked bed where Betty had died.

"Good Lord," Rev said after seeing the amount of blood.

Sandy nodded. "Yeah. We need to get *Mahi* down to Carlton's boatyard and get his guys working on ripping out and replacing all the carpet and the mattress. If she stays here, once the news gets out, she'll be a photo op for every creepy rubbernecker around, like those jerks I just ran off with the hose."

B2 looked worried. "Are you sure we should do that, Sandy? I mean, shouldn't his niece be the one to decide what gets done since she's his real family?"

Sandy shook his head. "She has enough to deal with right now, and I don't know how much she knows about boats. And face it, Baloney loved having *Mahi*'s picture taken because of the show. He'd hate to see that reason change because of what happened here last night. It's pretty clear that he won't be coming back anytime soon. But when he does come back—that's *when* and not *if* —I don't want him coming back to find *Mahi* looking like this. Agreed?"

Both men nodded. "I think he'd do the same thing for you, Sandy," Rev said.

"I know he would, Rev. How about you take your car and meet us up at *Albury's*? Bobby and I will bring *Mahi*. I'll handle the dock lines for you, Bobby, and then I'll call Carlton on the way."

FIVE MINUTES LATER, they were idling past the dock where *Oar House* was still tied up. Sandy had climbed up on the flybridge with B2, and from there, he noticed that both *Providence* and *Sandra T*'s slips were empty.

B2 said, "I wonder what'll happen to *Oar House*? I'm guessin' it was the owner that got killed."

"The cops aren't saying. But I have a feeling that somehow he was the reason for the attack on Betty and Bill. Maybe if he is dead, that reason might have gone away with him." It suddenly hit Sandy that this might not be true. He pulled out his phone and dialed Rikki Jenkins.

"Hey, Sandy."

"Hey, Rik. I was just thinking that whoever attacked Bill might come back and try to finish the job. Can you send somebody over to guard him in the hospital? I'll take care of the bill."

"Already done, Sandy; I sent someone over there right after we left. And there's no charge. I love that old curmudgeon too." She paused a second or two. "I'm going to bring Casey up to date on *Lady Dawn* in an hour about what I've found out if you want to sit in. Some things aren't good to be said over the phone."

"Roger that, Rik. B2, Rev, and I are taking *Mahi* over to Carlton's to get it off the dock and cleaned up. We'll be back at *Casey's Cove* at about the same time you will."

"Good deal. Bring them along too if they want to come."

"Will do. See you then."

RIKKI WAS ALREADY ABOARD and waiting in the salon when those three got back. They sat down across from Casey, Dawn, Kari, Marlin, and

Rikki, who were settled into two of the couches. Rikki leaned forward and began.

"For whatever reason, the Sheriff's Office seems to be dragging its heels on its investigation and is totally uncooperative with us. So we're working on it without their help. Even after they did the family notifications, they wouldn't tell us who was killed aboard *Oar House*. But we found out it was the owner, Steven Cohen, and a young woman named Chelsea Devine. They were attacked in a stateroom sometime around 4:00 a.m."

She was frustrated with what she considered her own team's progress being hampered by the sheriff and his outright dismissal of her offer of help. But there was even more to it, as she was about to reveal.

"Since Cohen and Devine were attacked first, we're assuming that they were the primary targets, either one or possibly both of them. But what's not clear is if they were, then why were Betty and Bill attacked? Neither of them had known Cohen for more than a day or two, and as far as we know, they had only met Devine on last night's cruise.

"Then there was that collision with the barge and the heated exchange with its crew, who both Angel and Debbie said sounded Asian. But according to the two women, they did not exchange names or any information, just insults. So, as far as we know, the crew of the barge had no way of knowing where *Oar House* was docked, especially since the prior owner's hailing port of Hampton hadn't yet been changed on the boat's stern.

"So, unless they had been in here over the last week or so, they wouldn't have that information. And Barry, the dockmaster, said he hadn't seen any barges around here lately, and the only Asians he's seen were aboard the *Sandra T*, and they're apparently Korean.

"That's an important distinction because the South Korean armed forces carry the Glock FM 78 field knife. The knife I saw the detective retrieve this morning at the hospital was a QNL-95 Chinese bayonet knife with rifle attachments. It is the one typically carried by the military of the People's Republic of China, something that no South Korean would ever carry.

"But here's something that can't leave this room; the knife I saw this morning is not the same knife that's in the evidence locker at the Sheriff's Office right now. I know this for a fact because it doesn't match the wounds on Betty or the two victims from *Oar House*. Somewhere between the hospital and the Coroner's Office, the knife got switched to a thin blade stiletto." It was obvious that Rikki had a confidential source in the Coroner's Office that was feeding her information.

"What the hell! Why would someone do that? Are you saying it was that detective?" Sandy was as shocked as everyone else.

"Either him or somebody at the SO. Whoever did it hadn't counted on the coroner trying to match the blade's shape to the wounds. They must've thought that since the lengths were the same, that was as far as they'd go to compare them."

Dawn asked, "Do you think the attacker might be someone in the Sheriff's Office?"

Rikki shook her head. "I don't think so; at least, I hope not. But that place has become so corrupt under Bromwell that I guess anything is possible. One thing is for certain; somebody over there is trying to cover the tracks of whoever murdered Betty. So, we can't trust anybody from the SO, especially Aldrich or Bromwell."

Marlin had been silent up until now. "Do you think you can figure out who killed Betty without any help from law enforcement?"

"I hope we'll be able to in spite of whoever at the SO is trying to sabotage their investigation. And we've still got one good hole card left in law enforcement—Stephanie." Special Agent Stephanie Baker of the FBI's Norfolk Field Office was another member of *Casey's Crew* and a friend of Baloney and Betty's.

"I spoke to her earlier, and she said her office is going to look into it quietly so as not to spook whoever did it. But she agreed; something over at the Northampton SO is rotten. As long as that person is still around, you can be sure their investigation will be going nowhere. Which is a plus for us. If that person knows the SO won't be coming up with any answers, they'll figure the same must be true with us. And I'm going to make certain that it isn't."

Sandy had been listening intently but now said, "Until you talked about the attacker using a Chinese military knife, I'd have been suspicious of this guy Han, who owns that electric-powered buyboat." He went on to describe Baloney's run-in with the man. "But it wasn't a big enough argument to get stabbed over."

"Still, that's good to know," Rikki said. "At this point, I'm not ready to rule many people out. Not yet."

~

MARLIN DENTON CALLED out from the finger pier, "You aboard, Sandy?"

"Yeah. Come on up, Marlin." He was sitting on the back deck, having a beer in the growing dusk. KC was curled up and asleep on Sandy's writing desk. "Grab a beer and a seat. I've been sitting here trying to gather my thoughts, and they aren't all that easy to round up right now. I feel like I've aged a decade since this morning."

"I can relate to that."

Marlin left that last part hanging, and Sandy could see he had something bothering him. Today, Sandy doubted that he knew anyone who didn't.

"Other than losing our sweet friend and Baloney now sitting in death's doorway with a homicidal maniac running around loose, what else is bothering you?"

Marlin sat down in a chair next to Sandy and looked down at his yet unopened beer. "I hope I didn't get Betty killed."

"What? Why on earth would you even think that's possible?"

"The show. I pushed Baloney into working on it, and he wasn't ready for how famous he got. If this was some crazy fan..."

"No, what's crazy is you thinking that you had anything at all to do with it. I'm not Rik, and I don't have her sense of deduction, but I'm willing to bet the show is not connected with it. The killer went onto *Oar House* first before *My Mahi*, and those two people had nothing to do with your show.

"You know better than anyone that Baloney getting cast in your show saved his butt. He'd stretched himself too thin, trying to rebuild *My Mahi*. He was about to lose it. They'd used up all their savings, and he badly underestimated what it would cost to get it running. That show became their life ring. Who would have figured that he would turn into such a cable sensation?"

"Not me. And that I'd end up having to renegotiate his contract with his manager to keep him on the show. Or that he'd even have a manager. It did turn out great in the end, though."

"Better than you know. It allowed him to bump B2 up from mate to captain, drastically improving Bobby's life. And Bill told me two days ago that he and Betty were planning the trip of a lifetime to London. They both were so excited. If there's any consolation to this, it's that she died in probably one of the happiest years of her life."

"Still, there should've been a lot more of those years." Marlin opened his beer and took a swig out of the bottle.

"Amen to that, friend."

"Any idea why the sheriff is dragging his heels on the investigation? Or if it's that detective?"

Sandy took his own swig of beer. "If I had to guess, I'd say the sheriff. The detective is just an incompetent son of a bitch. If Murph hadn't come up with that security video, I'd probably be sitting in a cell down at the SO right now. As to why drag their heels? It's been my experience that somebody is getting either paid or laid or wants to get either or both. Those are usually your two biggest reasons."

Marlin nodded. "All throughout time." He had another drink. "I really want to find this guy."

"No more than the rest of us. And we don't want him getting off on a technicality when we do."

"I don't know about you, but I'm willing to make certain that doesn't happen."

"Right there with you on that, brother."

They sat in silence, slowly draining their beers. Finally, Marlin stood up after finishing his. He asked, "You going to watch the launch?"

Sandy replied, "Didn't know there was going to be one."

"Yeah, a really big mother that should be spectacular. Some super-secret payload. Clear enough night, should be easy to watch. Take our minds off things for a while."

About eighty miles north of *Casey's Cove* on Wallops Island was the home of a NASA flight facility, one which launched all types of orbital and sub-orbital rockets and high-altitude flight experiments. These used to be mostly government payloads, but in recent years, more and more of the traffic had become commercial from the private sector. Many of the rocket launches were visible from *Casey's Cove*, especially the larger ones, like tonight's.

"What time, Marlin?"

"Around nine thirty."

"Doubtful. I want to be asleep, so I can try to escape from this nightmare for a while."

Marlin nodded. "I'm going to try to get some sleep, but I'm not sure that I can. I'd love to wake up tomorrow and find out this was all just a nightmare that didn't really happen."

"Yeah, me too."

8

COUNTDOWN

S aturday, 9:15 p.m., somewhere southeast of Wallops Island...

AS THE DRONE appeared from below on its custom-fitted elevator, he once again marveled at its design. He watched by the dim deck lights as the almost leathery-feeling wings automatically unrolled like a pair of ancient scrolls, finally taking a shape similar to that of a stingray. The result was a very large and ungainly-looking craft, but then, it never was designed to be graceful. Its six large, steerable electric motors would hover it only inches above the wave tops. This would keep it out of contact with the liquid domain of the string of hydrophones that were installed to detect any vessels that might be sneaking in downrange. Which was exactly why he and his launch vessel would not be there.

The large electric motors in the wings would be using a tremendous amount of energy, drawing down most of what was stored in the internal batteries by launch time. But these were only used to get it to the launch point, where the thin solid rocket booster in its belly would ignite. From that point on, the only electricity needed would be very minuscule, only enough to power the actuators in the wings that twist and change their aerodynamic shape, altering the course as necessary for the intercept.

There was one reason for the dual propulsion system, and that was to hide the original launch point—his vessel. Because if they were ever able to find him, they would have a clue that might begin to lead them back to the Supreme Leader in what would undoubtedly be deemed an act of war against the USA and one of its major allies.

This drone was a flying bomb, loaded with enough high explosives to rupture the fuel tanks and lines of the rocket, causing a catastrophic explosion. This would take out its payload of four spy satellites which were scheduled to replace their older, failing counterparts, leaving the South as well as the West virtually blind to what the Supreme Leader was planning. By the time new replacement satellites were built and launched, it would already be too late to stop things once the plan was discovered.

To be certain, there was a lot of new technology aboard the drone, and it all had to work flawlessly if this was to be a success. But the systems had all been tested time and again. If all went as planned, the drone would go into autonomous mode once it was launched, skimming above the waves until it held steady "on station," matching the motion of the waves. The leathery material would absorb most radar signals, and even if it was spotted intermittently, at almost surface height, its low profile would likely be mistaken for floating debris.

Once the drone's infrared system detected the heat bloom of the rocket's engine firing, its own solid rocket would ignite, climbing and intercepting the rocket before it was able to reach supersonic speed. The combined explosion should eliminate most of the drone, scattering whatever bits were left downrange in the ocean along with the rocket and satellite pieces.

Should the launch be postponed and the drone's batteries drained down to a critical level, it would seek out an infrared homing signal from its launch vessel, returning for a rapid recharge. This was the only communication available between the drone and the launch vessel since radio silence was crucial to the stealth aspect of the mission. The use of infrared communication was chosen because, unlike radio, it couldn't be jammed and was far less likely to be detected.

As the rocket's launch time approached, the launch team on the boat worked their way down a simple checklist. One quick visual scan of the area revealed the lights of a couple of other boats that were also outside of the exclusionary security zone. Beyond them were several blue strobe lights of the patrol boats. All looked normal, so he gave the order to launch. The drone lifted up and off the elevator, disappearing into the dark night. If all went as planned, it would be the last time that he would see the automated vehicle.

TYRELL GRAFTON SAT in a chair just inside the doorway of the surgical intensive care unit waiting room. From here, he had a clear view of the only doorway leading into the SICU, as well as some of the hallway leading up to it. This wasn't as close as he'd have liked to have been, but it was as close as the hospital would allow. They'd insisted their own security was more than adequate to protect Bill Cooper, even though this amounted to a lone guard who walked past the SICU doorway twice an hour. They argued that the Sheriff's Office hadn't even seen the need to post one of their deputies on site, so they failed to see the need for any private security.

After a call from Rikki Jenkins, this was the compromise they'd been able to work out. Tyrell and the agent who would be relieving him could keep watch from this position. The only people other than close relatives of the other two patients currently in the SICU who would be allowed in were hospital employees with photo IDs clipped to the front of their scrubs. Meaning that all the security agents must stay out of the SICU itself and out of the way of its staff.

Since the hospital operated on twelve-hour shifts, Tyrell had quickly identified most of the people who routinely came and went from the SICU. As it was almost 10:00 p.m., the waiting room was empty, though it would no doubt get busy at some point tomorrow morning. Until then, the solitude made it that much easier for him to concentrate on his job.

Word must have gotten around to the staff, and most were now giving him friendly nods as they passed, realizing that he was protection for them as well in the event of an incident. Hopefully, the night would pass quietly.

Tyrell decided to walk down the hall to the nearest coffee machine to grab his first cup of what would probably be several over the next few hours. Fortunately, the machine was still in sight of the SICU doorway, about twenty yards away. He passed an orderly as he zeroed in on the beloved caffeine dispenser. He'd only gone a few steps farther when it hit him that something wasn't right about the guy. He was dressed in the usual scrubs that were the common uniform, as well as a disposable hairnet and face mask. But he was also wearing nitrile gloves, which were usually donned right before performing some procedure, not when taking a stroll down the hallway. And his badge was clipped on backward, with the photo facing inward toward his scrubs.

Tyrell turned back around just as the man was disappearing through the doorway into the SICU. That brief glimpse also revealed that he had a long black braided ponytail that reached halfway down his back. And unlike the clogs favored by so many of the hospital staff, the man was wearing black tactical boots.

Tyrell raced down the hall and through the SICU doorway, but the man was nowhere in sight. One of the startled nurses began to object, telling him that he couldn't be in there until she saw the SIG Sauer pistol up and in his hand. He knew exactly where the man was headed, and he rushed over and yanked back the curtain on Baloney's room. The man had a combat knife raised chest-high, preparing to plunge it down into Baloney's heart. Without a word, Tyrell shot the man twice in the side of his chest, causing him to twist away from Baloney, but he still didn't go down. One more shot, this time into his heart, sent the man reeling backward into Baloney's IV fluid tree and finally down onto the floor.

FROM A DISTANCE of a couple of miles, the drone's launch team watched as the rocket's flaming exhaust illuminated the coast of Wallops Island like daylight. Only by knowing where to look were they able to detect the much smaller flame from the drone as it began its ascent. In seconds, the sky was filled with flaming debris and burning rocket fuel right before the sound and concussion of the explosion reached their boat.

The man smiled, then said to the crewman next to him, "We must not leave for several minutes. Doing so would only cause suspicion. We will go when we see the other boats leave that were also watching."

He was elated over their success. But before the daylight broke, he would learn how badly the rest of the night had gone. Meanwhile, though, he had to make a quick stop to offload the drone elevator. If it were sitting on the barge, it would look like just another unique piece of marine construction equipment. But aboard his boat, it would be hard to explain. Hopefully, tonight there wouldn't be any further complications like yesterday's when the boat had been forced to return to pick up the equipment after almost getting caught.

RIKKI HAD ARRIVED and received a quick briefing from Tyrell in the SICU waiting room. He told her that the SICU staff had already moved Baloney into another room while leaving the rest of the scene intact. A deputy had questioned him there briefly, confiscating his pistol before ushering him out and across the hallway. He then told him not to go anywhere before a detective had a chance to question him more in-depth. But before being forced out of the SICU, Tyrell had watched two crime scene techs taking photos of the room and the dead assassin. One had pulled up the dead man's sleeves, revealing several tattoos, and the other had removed the man's surgical mask, revealing his Asian features.

"Rikki, the guy's a Triad; I saw the triangle tattoo on his forearm when they were photographing him."

The Triads were a transnational organized crime syndicate whose roots were in mainland China, with tentacles reaching into Macau, Taiwan, Hong Kong, Australia, Europe, and North and South America. They had now established a presence on the Eastern Shore, with this cell being run by its creator, a man known locally only as Fong.

The news about the assassin's affiliation took Rikki by surprise, but only for a second, as things began to click together in her mind. She nodded. As she was about to reply, they heard an angry voice from the hallway.

"Hey! You get the hell away from my detainee!" Sheriff Bromwell had arrived with Detective Aldrich in tow. "Detective, you go question that man while I have a little chat with Ms. Jenkins here."

Aldrich led Tyrell over to a far corner of the room as Bromwell got into Rikki's face. "You are interfering in a criminal investigation, and if you don't back off, I'll arrest your skinny little ass, Jenkins. I don't give a damn who's on your client list; they ain't gonna do you any good when you're locked in a cell with no phone."

"Sorry we took so long, boss. The deputies didn't want to let us through until there were more of us than them." Four of Rikki's agents now arrived in the room and were beginning to surround the sheriff.

Rikki smiled at Bromwell. "I haven't broken any laws, and you're damn well not going to take me anywhere unless I do." She watched over his shoulder as a deputy took Tyrell's SIG over to Aldrich in a plastic evidence bag. "And his nine-millimeter better not magically change and turn into a thirty-eight between here and your office like that knife changed."

Rikki had deliberately said that last part loud enough for Aldrich to hear. She watched him turn and give her a questioning look. On the other hand, Bromwell looked startled. She was sure she had her answer.

The sheriff recovered quickly. "I don't know what the hell you're talking about! And you and your men need to clear out of here."

"Neither do I, but I'd sure love to hear about it. Since you didn't see the need to protect a witness, Sheriff, you should be thanking her that she did, or you'd have a hell of a lot of explaining to do. Then again, you still might." Stephanie Baker had arrived, along with Casey Shaw and Sandy Morgan.

The sheriff's eyes started darting around as if assessing his odds since the opposing group was growing rapidly. That, or he might be formulating a possible escape route. Then he glared at Stephanie. "The FBI hasn't got jurisdiction here; this is a county matter. So why don't you get the hell out and take Jenkins and her crew with you."

"We have jurisdiction wherever I say we do, especially when these events may also be connected with a parallel investigation." She watched his face closely as some of the color drained from it. "We need Captain Cooper to be protected as well, and since you aren't willing to, and the hospital isn't capable of it, I think a proven federal contractor like ESVA Security is an excellent choice for the job. Especially since a group other than Uncle Sam is picking up the tab."

The sheriff snapped back, "Not while someone from ESVA Security is under suspicion of murder."

The normally cool-headed Rikki exploded. "Murder? That's exactly what he prevented; no thanks to you! And why was that? Maybe you need to answer a few questions of your own. Maybe we should skip right on past the State Police and go straight to the Department of Justice if that's what you want. Or maybe that is what Special Agent Baker was alluding to."

More color drained out of Bromwell's face as Stephanie shot Rikki a silent "Don't say anything more" look. Something that wasn't lost on the sheriff.

Bromwell quickly recovered and said, "Let's hold on a second here, Agent Baker; you may have a point. Ain't no sense in starting a jurisdictional pissing match over who gets to babysit Cooper. My department is stretched mighty thin right now investigating these murders. If you're willing to take responsibility for Cooper's security, I don't care if you want to sign off on Jenkins's group; that's your business. But it'll be your ass if they screw it up."

Stephanie said, "Seeing as they already saved your ass tonight by saving Cooper's, I'd say they'll do just fine." She looked straight into his eyes, "I'm assuming that you'll put your best people on investigating this latest attack and identifying the attacker and any group or accomplices he might be connected to."

He scowled and said, "Don't you try tellin' me how to do my job, Baker. And you, Jenkins, you and your people stay the hell out of the way of my investigation, or you're gonna see the inside of one of my cells." He shoved one of Rikki's agents back out of his path as he went out into the hall.

Aldrich was just finishing up with Tyrell and quickly followed the sheriff out. Tyrell walked back over to Rikki. She asked, "How'd that go?"

"About like you'd expect. That guy isn't the brightest, but at least his questions were straightforward. Wants me to go to the SO in the morning and give a formal statement."

She nodded. "And our lawyer is going with you. There's a lot going on behind the curtain right now, and we aren't sure what that is or who is playing on whose team."

"I kind of figured that. Thanks for the lawyer."

"Thanks for saving my friend. Go home and get some rest. Jeff, you drive Tyrell home in his car, and Paul, you follow and bring Jeff back."

Tyrell said, "Thanks, Rikki."

Rikki motioned to Stephanie, Sandy, and Casey for them to follow over to the far corner of the room, where they each took a seat. "Steph, are you really running a parallel investigation?"

She gave a sly smile. "Not yet, but I'm beginning to think it's not a bad idea. But it'll have to wait until this other situation settles down; they've tasked everybody on this, and I've got to get up there."

Casey had kept quiet, but he spoke up now, asking, "What situation?"

"A rocket exploded up at Wallops."

Rikki looked confused. "Since when are you with NASA?"

"I've told you all I can about it."

Casey said, "We can get that much off the television. So, you guys must think it had some help. What kind of rocket? What was it carrying?"

"I'd tell you more if I could, but I can't."

To avoid any further awkward conversation, Rikki changed the subject back to the attacks. She filled Stephanie in as much as she could about the knife swap without revealing her source. Then she told her about the sheriff's reaction.

"Oh yeah, we'll be digging into this ASAP. Thanks, Rik."

"No, thank you for coming tonight. Things were about to get ugly until you showed up. Bromwell is definitely afraid of the Feds."

"Sure seemed that way."

Rikki said, "Case, we need to find that barge *Oar House* hit as soon as we can."

"Wait, what? Why?"

"Because whoever was on it was speaking in some kind of Asian language and was pretty upset over having been hit. A few hours later, the only two people left aboard *Oar House* are dead, and then Betty and Bill are attacked by someone using that Chinese military knife. And tonight, less than twenty-four hours later, a Triad member tries to kill him again."

"Triad? Are you certain?" Stephanie asked.

"Tyrell saw the guy's forearm tattoo. You know, the triangle with a Chinese symbol inside of it. You won't live very long on the street with one of those if you aren't a gang member."

"Very true."

Casey spoke up. "We can take the seaplane in the morning; that way, we can cover a lot of territory fast."

Rikki had recently taken a single-engine Cessna Grand Caravan turboprop seaplane as payment for an asset recovery job. She'd traded it for shares in Casey and Dawn's Shaw Air charter business.

Stephanie sounded worried. "You two better be careful. This whole thing sounds crazy, but on the off chance that the barge is related to the attacks and if it belongs to the Triad, you could be flying into a hornet's nest. If you find it, don't screw around; call me immediately."

Casey nodded. "Roger that."

"WE HAVE A PROBLEM."

"I don't pay you to tell me about problems; I pay you to fix them."

"Yeah, well, this was one that your boy created."

"What do you mean?"

"The guy you sent screwed up the job. Totally missed him and got shot and killed in the process."

"Who killed him? You were supposed to make sure there weren't to be any deputies there, and hospital security does not carry guns."

"Private security, sent by Jenkins and Shaw. Then the FBI showed up…"

"WHAT! FBI? Who called them in?"

"Probably Jenkins. She's tight with the Feds and friends with this Agent Baker woman. I heard her mention some kind of parallel investigation, but she didn't say into what."

The silence on the phone was deafening for a few seconds. "So, they have seen his tattoos." It was intended as both a statement and a question.

"Yeah. Nothing I could have done about that. But I'll stall any specific identification as long as I can."

"Indefinitely."

"Like I said, as long as I can, but this is getting to be a big mess, and now it's going beyond the department."

"Indefinitely, or it may be you they identify next."

The statement shook him. "All right, I'll do what I can, but no guarantees."

Silence.

"Hello?"

That's when he realized the person on the other phone had already hung up.

9

———

THE HORNET'S NEST

Sunday, 5:30 a.m., Accomack County Airport, ESVA

CASEY WAS COMPLETING the exterior preflight check of the Caravan when Rikki arrived with two large paper cups of coffee, handing one to him.

"Good morning, Case."

"It is now. I overslept and didn't get a chance to have a cup before I left. No coffee makes for a slow start."

Rikki nodded. "I called the hospital, there's no change in Bill's condition, but at least he's still with us. They wouldn't tell me anything more. Only immediate family get detailed updates, and that means Debbie... and Sandy."

"Sandy?"

"He's got them believing that he and Bill are related." She grinned.

"That'll be a good story to tell him when..." Casey stopped, not wanting to tempt the Fates by finishing the sentence with, "...he gets back home." There were still a lot of hurdles to leap over before Baloney could get to that point.

Rikki quickly asked, "So, where do you think this thing is?"

Casey shook his head, bringing his thoughts back into focus on the task at hand. "I'm guessing somewhere off Cobb or Hog Islands. They were supposed to be on a booze cruise, and Bill wouldn't be running an unfamiliar boat very fast after dark. Unfortunately, he's the only one who would know exactly where the barge was anchored. But it's not like there are going to be dozens of barges anchored up out there if it's even still in the area. But they were only gone a few hours, and at cruising speed, that wouldn't take them too far beyond North Inlet before he'd have turned around.

"It's curious, though, that any barge would be left anchored out in the ocean, even at this time of year when the water's generally flatter than in winter. No way to leave one out there at that time of year. Makes me wonder what it was doing out there in unsheltered water in the first place, Rik."

"I have no idea. But it has to be related to what got Betty killed, though I still don't know how whoever the murderer was knew where she and Bill lived and where *Oar House* docked. I don't buy that they were all attacked just because they ran into an anchored barge. And why would anyone be staying on such an unlit hazard to navigation after dark like that? Makes zero sense."

"Well, the sun's already coming up, and we won't get any answers here. Let's go find that thing."

AT THAT SAME MOMENT, two figures were climbing back down into a small rigid hull outboard inflatable boat after delivering their cargo. Backing away rapidly, the captain set a course south to the Great North Inlet. He went to wide-open throttle on the tiller arm outboard, skimming across the flat-calm ocean.

ONCE AIRBORNE, Casey turned the plane east and then south after he intercepted the coastline. They passed over *The Bluffs* at a low altitude. This was another restaurant and marina complex their investment group owned.

Rikki commented, "The marina looks pretty full, and the deck is packed."

"Flounder season, so it better be, or we'll be in trouble. Hey, have you heard anything more from Stephanie this morning? I'm wondering what she's going to do about that knife swap."

"I'm sure she's going to dig into it after they get finished with that rocket sabotage case."

"So, it was definitely sabotaged?"

"Yep. I made a few calls on my way home. Everybody is pretty tight-lipped, so how it was done has everybody spooked."

Casey was intrigued. "How did it happen?"

"They aren't certain; that's what has them so spooked. Some kind of missile appeared out of thin air in the restricted zone. Came up from the ocean's surface."

"Boat- or submersible-launched?"

Rikki shook her head. "Couldn't have been. They didn't pick up anything on the radar or the sonar net. Some kind of freaking Houdini act."

Casey went silent as he began scanning the coastline. From 1,500 feet on this clear day, they could see for several miles. He spotted something in the distance just off Hog Island.

"That might be our barge. I'm going to take us lower so we can get a better look." He pushed the nose down, gaining speed and losing altitude. The object was about three miles away, and by the time they reached it, they had already positively confirmed it as a barge.

Casey had brought them down to just under one hundred feet above the ocean's surface. As they blew past the barge about fifty feet off its offshore side, Rikki videoed it with her phone. It was indeed an old, rusty, steel work barge, about 120 feet long by twenty-five feet wide. Its deck was about three and a half feet above the water, and it had a short, thin white streak on its rounded top edge, about in the middle where *Oar House* had hit it at a glancing blow.

Other than the usual small construction debris commonly found on work barges, the only thing on the deck was an old steel cargo container. Its doors were closed, and the barge seemed deserted.

Rikki asked, "Can we go back and land next to it? I'd like to board it if we can."

"Not a problem, Rik. I'll land on the inshore side of it and let the barge act as a breakwater for any offshore boat wakes. It's low enough that we can pull up right alongside."

"Great. You're carrying, right?"

"Oh, hell, yes. Glock 19. Fifteen rounds in the magazine and one in the pipe."

"Here's hoping you won't need that first one, but something about this doesn't feel right."

"I have that same feeling you do. The hair is standing up on my neck."

Casey circled back around the barge, then set up on a straight-in approach that would bring them alongside it. When the floats came in contact with the water, he held his speed up, keeping the plane "on step" until they got closer. Then he throttled back, allowing the floats to settle into the water as he idled up alongside.

The deck was indeed low enough to allow the plane's wing to overlap it. Rikki lassoed a cleat on the barge from atop a float with one of the plane's dock lines. She quickly secured the plane with it and climbed onto the barge, followed by Casey. Another visual scan showed there was no one in sight, and the doors to the container were latched shut from the outside. There were two raised three-foot-square access hatches in the deck, which led down into the bilge, and they were also shut.

Rikki silently pointed to the container as she pulled her gun from her back holster, and Casey did the same. They crept forward slowly, then Rikki unlatched the first door, which opened with a loud creak. She used the door as a shield as she peered around it into the dark recess of the large steel box.

"Clear, Case. Open that other half, will you? We need more light."

As Casey unlatched and opened the second door, allowing in more of the early dawn light, Rikki replaced her pistol and pulled out her phone again. She videoed what appeared to be a strange steel framework similar to a small construction scissor lift. It sat on a wheeled dolly in the middle of the otherwise empty container. She made her way to the back of the container, still videoing. Casey was walking in when Rikki spotted something under the lift that made her blood go cold.

Rikki yelled, "Case, let's get out of here! Bomb!"

Casey didn't need any more urging as he silently turned and sprinted out of the container and over to the plane. As he dove through the pilot's door, he yelled, "Rik, get that line, and I'll get us cranked up!"

The turboprop was already spooling up as Rikki began to untie them. She hadn't made it onto the float before an explosion somewhere in the bilge shook the barge. Both of the heavy steel access hatches in the deck blew straight up into the air. One landed inches away from the leading edge of the plane's wing. The concussion reverberated through the steel deck like a drum skin. The energy from the explosion transferred up into her legs and knocked her overboard, where she landed on her stomach on the float, stunning her.

Through the open passenger door, she heard Casey yelling, "Rik! Are you okay? Rik!"

As she struggled up onto her feet on the float, she yelled back, "Go, go, go!" She began clawing her way through the doorway on her stomach, pulling herself forward as Casey hit the throttle. The thrust from the propeller and their increasing speed pinned the door against her legs, which were still sticking outside. She wriggled and squirmed, finally grabbing the rear support of one of the seats, gathering herself in farther by pulling against it.

Rikki managed to get one foot all the way inside and then used it to push against the door, freeing her other leg and pulling it into the cabin. She reached over, latched the door, and stood up as Casey climbed and banked the plane.

Looking out the window and back at the barge, she had the presence of mind to pull out her phone and continue videoing. It was now down at the bow, the deck less than a foot above the water. The bomb must have ripped a huge hole in the hull.

As she watched, two simultaneous explosions occurred, one again somewhere in the bilge, this time at the stern. But a much larger one happened inside the container, shredding the metal sides and roof. It turned them into a lethal spray of shrapnel and left a gaping hole in the deck where it had been sitting. Even as far away as they were, the concussion still shook the airplane and spread outward in a concentric circle across the surface of the water. The smoke from the explosion had cleared slightly right before what was left of the hull slipped beneath the water, leaving only a handful of floating debris and a small oil slick.

Rikki made her way back up to the co-pilot's seat. Casey looked her over and asked, "Are you all right?"

"Probably be a little sore tomorrow, but I'll live. And I'd say we got our answer."

"What answer? We nearly got killed! If we'd gotten into that container a minute later…"

"But we didn't, and we're still alive. The answer we got is that whatever that thing was in the container apparently must've been worth killing for. Whoever had it went to a lot of trouble to get rid of it. It was on wheels, and they could've easily pushed it over the side. Instead, they put one big-assed bomb under it to blow it to smithereens. And they scuttled the barge itself with not one but two charges. We're lucky that they didn't all go off at one time or that the container wasn't the first to blow. Damned lucky." She began making a call.

"Who're you calling?"

"Stephanie. She said to call if we found it."

"If I remember correctly, she said to call *immediately* if we found it."

"Oops. So, I'm a little late calling her. If we'd just circled over it, we'd have had no idea what was in that container."

Casey said, "Well, when you think about it, we still don't know."

"Kind of true... Hey, Stephanie, we found the barge... Yeah, slight problem with that; it's gone... blew up... Not before we got aboard and shot some video. Found a very strange looking... I can email it to... Okay. About twenty minutes, but that's a restricted... Okay, see you then."

"What did she say?"

"She wants us up at Wallops Island ASAP."

"That airstrip is restricted."

"We're already cleared."

THE AIRFIELD at NASA's Wallops Island Flight Facility was located on the main part of the Eastern Shore. It was separated from the spaceport over on the coast by a lot of marsh and water. There was a causeway through the marsh and a bridge over the navigable water of Cat Creek.

Even though they were heading to the airfield, Casey and Rikki could see the launch pad and its related facilities. There was also a small armada of Navy and Coast Guard ships just offshore, apparently stationed along the downrange flight path, recovering pieces of the rocket from the seafloor.

Casey was directed by the tower to land on runway four. Utilizing the reverse pitch of the turboprop's propeller, he was able to stop short of an intersecting runway. He was then directed to take a taxiway over to a large, dilapidated-looking hangar where Stephanie Baker waited outside on the tarmac. She walked straight over to Rikki with a very tired and serious look on her face.

She held her hand out, frowning. "You were supposed to call me when you found it. Let me see the video." After watching it once, she looked up and said, "You two were damned lucky."

Casey said, "Believe me, we're both very aware of that. But why did you want us to bring that video in person rather than just emailing it to you?"

"For the same reason that you're going to be sworn to secrecy and not allowed to tell anyone else about its existence or what you saw on that barge. Come with me."

She led them over toward the hangar door just as a large military helicopter approached the tarmac. A huge cargo net was hanging below it, filled with pieces of twisted metal. A forklift and several men in uniform rushed past them from out of the hangar. The men were pushing wheeled carts.

As they went through the door, Rikki asked, "So, you think the barge and the missile that took down the rocket are related?"

Stephanie's head spun in her direction. "How'd you know about... oh, right, it's you. Never mind. Let's just say that two large explosions this close together within a few hours of each other in a relatively uninhabited part of the country... it's unlikely to be a coincidence."

Ahead of them, in the large hangar, several people were placing recovered parts of the rocket jigsaw puzzle together in an effort to determine where and how it was hit. Stephanie signaled to one of them, a man who looked to be in his middle fifties. He pointed to a door over at the side as he started walking toward it. The trio went over to it as well. Inside was a briefing room with a conference table and a large flat-screen monitor.

"This is Dr. Werner Beck," Stephanie said. "He's an explosives expert." She handed him Rikki's phone, which he wirelessly connected to the flat screen. Instantly, the beginning scenes of the video appeared. When they reached the point where they were inside the container, he froze the video several times.

"This is some kind of munitions elevator, but it's not like any I've seen before. Most are self-propelled and have their own onboard battery power. This is neither. Note that it is sitting on a manually pushed dolly of some sort. See the plates with the holes at the bottom of all four corners? It was mounted somewhere, and they didn't want it moving.

"Look at the size of those cables; they were meant to carry a lot of amperage. This plugs into some kind of electrical source and runs to the lift motor here," he pointed at a spot on the screen. "But it splits off from there and goes to this high amperage plug at the end of this short cord. So, it was feeding something, and that something needed a hell of a lot of juice. Did you see anything else in or near the container?"

When both Casey and Rikki shook their heads, he said, "My best guess is that it was removed from a large boat. Something innocuous and much larger than an outboard. This lift itself weighs quite a lot. Or, rather, it *weighed* quite a lot. And see the size and material of that bomb? This isn't homegrown fertilizer and fuel oil. This is high-grade military spec stuff. You don't go down to the local hardware store and get this. That lift was custom-made as well."

Casey spoke up. "This makes no sense. Even if our friends on *Oar House* saw this sitting out on the deck, they wouldn't have any clue what it was."

Beck looked blankly at Stephanie, "*Oar House*? What friends?"

She gave him a quick overview; then he looked at Casey and Rikki with a sincere face. "My condolences. I agree with you; they wouldn't have had any clue about it if this was all they'd seen. But if they saw the delivery device with it, that might've been a different story."

"If Baloney had seen anything out of the ordinary, he'd probably have been telling everybody back at the docks about it," Rikki said.

"Baloney?" Beck asked.

Stephanie said, "Long story. But whoever did this"—she motioned toward the hanger where the pieces were being reassembled—"is going to great lengths to tie up loose ends. Cohen, Devine, and Baloney all interacted with the people on that barge and might have seen their faces, making each of them a liability."

Rikki argued, "So how did they know where to find them?"

Stephanie shrugged. "I'm only offering theories, not all the answers. Those are what we need to find."

"I'm going to want to recover as much evidence as possible from the blast. If we send you two down there in a helicopter, do you think you can pinpoint the location where the barge sank and drop a buoy there? Any idea how deep it is?"

Casey said, "Yes, we can, and somewhere around thirty and forty feet."

"Then let's get you two going. And I'll have a recovery ship head that way ASAP. The longer those pieces stay in the water, there will be less of any trace of the explosives that might be left on them."

FLYING to the site in a Sikorsky Seahawk helicopter, Casey and Rikki were able to identify the approximate position of the wrecked barge. Due to the murky blue-green water, there wasn't enough visibility to spot any wreckage on the bottom from up in the air. But the helicopter was also carrying a lightweight underwater magnetometer capable of finding objects up to 1,500 feet to either side of it. The lightweight torpedo-shaped detector spotted the wreck in the first two minutes of being dragged underwater behind the helicopter. The crew noted the GPS coordinates, then tossed an orange plastic buoy with a long line and anchor next to it before returning their passengers back to Wallops. Again, Stephanie was waiting on the concrete ramp.

"There's someone here who needs to talk to both of you."

They were led back to the same briefing room, only this time, there was another man inside, and he was wearing a suit. He was from an agency that Casey had never heard of but that Rikki's company had done work for in the past. He told them this was all now a matter of national security and swore them to secrecy, explaining the harsh penalties that could befall them if they chose to break that oath.

"What about the safety of my friend, Bill Cooper? If this is all linked, shouldn't he be guarded by some federal agency?" Casey asked.

Stephanie answered, "We'll be picking up your bill, Rik, but that also needs to be kept confidential. We need you to continue your protection detail as normal. If we suddenly pulled your team and replaced it with federal agents, I guarantee that word would get out, and it would alert the wrong people. The way it is now, it just looks like his wealthy friends are paying to protect their friend."

"So then, you're thinking the local law enforcement might be part of this and directly involved in a wider conspiracy," Casey stated.

"Right now, Case, we aren't ruling anything or anyone out. We're watching a few persons of interest, and that's all I can say about it."

Stephanie handed Rikki's phone back to her. Checking her history, Rikki noted the video had been erased after undoubtedly being uploaded to some secure server somewhere.

"Remember, you two, not a word about any of this to anyone. And trust no one in your local law enforcement agencies. If you see or hear anything suspicious, call me immediately, no matter how small a detail it is. Keep your eyes open, your guard up, and your firearms locked and loaded."

10

THROUGH THE FOG

Baloney was navigating his way through the thick fog. But this wasn't like the thick winter fog on the Chesapeake; this was far more dense and almost seemed alive. He heard voices coming from inside of it, a pair of Asian voices, and they were angry. He couldn't understand what they were saying, nor could he see the faces or the bodies of whoever was doing the talking, and soon they drifted away. As they did, he suddenly saw the stern of a boat disappearing into the dark mist. It looked so familiar, but he couldn't quite place it.

From somewhere in the mist, he now heard a familiar, comforting voice; *Hang in there, Gilligan. We're all pulling for you.* It took every ounce of strength he had, but he answered quietly before being hit with a sudden, intense pain that seemed to come from everywhere within his chest. He fell backward into that dark mist, only this time, it was comforting, and the pain faded away.

APPARENTLY, Baloney was making progress. They had removed his breathing tube and replaced it with a nasal cannula delivering oxygen to his nostrils so his face wasn't quite as obscured. Though he still looked bad, almost lifeless. Sandy looked at his watch, knowing the nurse would be kicking him out in the next minute or two. He leaned forward, speaking softly into Baloney's ear. "Hang in there, Gilligan. We're all pulling for you." He leaned back and prepared to leave when he heard an almost whispered, very hoarse reply, "Hack."

Sandy couldn't have been more shocked if he'd been hit with a cattle prod. "What? What did you say, Gilligan?" But there was no additional reply, and Baloney's face looked as waxy and ashen as it had since he'd come out of surgery.

"Time to go, Mr. Morgan." The nurse had appeared and gently lay a hand on his arm.

"He just said something! He heard me talk to him, and he responded! That's good, right?"

The nurse pushed past him, glancing at the monitors and placing a stethoscope diaphragm on Baloney's chest. "You're sure he said something? He's still pretty sedated."

"Yes! He called me by my nickname. I didn't imagine it!"

Then she held Baloney's wrist as she physically checked his pulse. She smiled as she looked up. "I'd say that's a very good sign."

SANDY WALKED BACK to the waiting room, feeling like a condemned man who'd just received a pardon. Casey had arrived, waiting for an update, and was sitting in a chair. Other than a couple of Rikki's agents, he was the only other person in the room. He looked hopeful as he stared at Sandy.

"You're smiling?"

"Bill talked to me! It was only one word, and he never opened his eyes, but he responded to me and called me 'Hack.' I never thought I'd like to hear that nickname, but I was beginning to doubt that I ever would again. The nurse says it's a good sign."

"Heck yes, I'll take it as a great sign! That's the best news I've heard all day."

Sandy took a chair next to Casey and said, "Now I know he's going to pull through. Hearing that was the best feeling I've had since he was brought in here."

Casey nodded. "Me too."

"The nurse was surprised he could say anything because he's still sedated."

"Well, if the doctors knew Bill like we do, they'd have doubled the dosage. You can't go by body weight or height with him; it's more about toughness and sheer will."

Sandy chuckled. "Also known as stubbornness."

"Pretty much," Casey agreed.

The two were silent a few moments before Sandy leaned forward in his chair and asked, "So, how'd your expedition go? Dawn told me you and Rik were searching for that barge with the seaplane. Did you find it?"

"We did."

"Did you get aboard? Did you find anything?"

"I can't talk about it."

That took Sandy aback. "What do you mean you can't talk about it?"

"Just what I said. I'm *not allowed* to talk about it."

"Who won't let you talk about it?"

"I can't tell you that, either."

Sandy blinked several times, trying hard to comprehend what Casey was really saying. Not the part about not talking; that was clear enough. But he knew Casey wanted him to read between the lines for the answers he wasn't allowed to give. On a hunch, he asked, "Did you happen to see or talk to Stephanie this morning?"

A sly smile appeared on Casey's face. He'd known Sandy would get it. "I might have seen her."

"Wasn't she up at Wallops? Wouldn't they have that locked down to visitors now?"

Casey smiled and shrugged.

"You went there?"

The shrug was back.

Sandy thought aloud, "So, why would the FBI want to talk to you in person bad enough to have you go into a locked-down complex? Maybe because they didn't want you talking over the phone?"

"I didn't say that."

"You aren't denying it either."

Another shrug.

Sandy's face clouded. "So, that barge is definitely linked to what happened at *Mallard Cove*."

Silence.

"I liked you better when you could talk."

Casey nodded. "So did I."

"This means that Baloney is still in danger."

"Let's just say that Rik's team won't be leaving anytime soon."

"There must have been something or someone on that barge that they saw, or somebody thinks they saw. Enough to kill for. Then the next day, sixty miles north, somebody brings down a rocket with a payload that Stephanie couldn't talk about last night. And these things are all linked together."

Casey stayed mute, but Sandy could see by the look in his eyes that he was right. It frustrated him that they couldn't just talk about it, but he knew Casey would have a good reason as to why he couldn't. He decided that thinking aloud some more might help bring things into focus.

"There were Asian-sounding people on the barge. And a Triad member tried to kill Baloney this time, so we can assume those things are probably linked. But why would the Triad want to bring down a rocket? Do they even have the know-how and expertise required? I thought they were more into smuggling dope and selling human slaves.

"According to the paper this morning, that was one of the biggest rockets that can be launched from Wallops. The kind that can carry cargo to a space station or put several satellites into orbit at one time. Neither of those things would have anything to do with the Triad. None of this makes any sense."

After being so overjoyed at hearing Baloney's voice again, Sandy's elation began switching over to confusion, frustration, and anger. All these emotions now collided with the memory of the past two days' events. He began pacing back and forth as he talked.

"Someone or some group killed Betty and those other two people for what? Then they tried to kill Baloney twice. Who? Some street gang? I don't buy that; street gangs don't take down rockets or own barges. We need to find out who is really behind this and put a stop to it. Or is Baloney supposed to live the rest of his life with a security team? We need to figure out what he, Betty, and those other two saw that was so threatening to someone or some group."

Casey stood up and put a hand on his friend's shoulder, stopping his pacing.

"Sandy, we need to trust Stephanie and let her do her job. If anyone can get to the bottom of this, it's her. And we both know she's not afraid to shoot when the situation calls for it. If she were, I wouldn't still be alive. Let's go back to the *Cove*, and I'll buy you lunch."

"No thanks, I'm staying here until the next visiting period in forty-five minutes. I want to see if he's able to talk again."

"Then we'll both stay."

DEBBIE SHOWED up right before the visiting time, so she and Sandy went in together. They weren't as lucky this time since Baloney didn't say a word. When the nurse came in to tell them visiting time had expired, she reminded both not to read too much into his silence.

"It was amazing that he said anything this soon. I wouldn't expect him to be able to talk again for another day or two when we start weaning him off the sedation. We don't want him fighting it. His body has been through so much, and talking uses up the strength that it needs to heal itself. He's making amazing progress but still has a long way to go. You two might want to go home and get some rest until tomorrow. He won't know that you weren't here. If anything changes or if he wakes up, we'll call you."

Reluctantly, the two agreed and left.

.   .   .

SANDY FOLLOWED Casey back to the *Mallard Cove Restaurant* for lunch out on the back deck. It was usual to see some, if not all, of the charter boats' slips empty this time of day. But the empty one behind the sign for *My Mahi* was a grim reminder of their lost friend and their other friend who was fighting to stay in this world.

Climbing the short flight of stairs, they spotted Eric and Han having lunch together across the deck. Eric gave them a slight wave.

Sandy commented, "Interesting lunch-mates, those two."

"Maybe not. I heard that Eric is interested in Han's electric drive setup, and Han is interested in Eric's emulsion unit. Reasonable to assume they'd chat over lunch."

"I guess." Something about the pair bothered Sandy, though he couldn't put his finger on exactly what it was. Maybe because the last time he'd seen Han, he was in a shouting match with Baloney. While it was true that the man was Asian, Baloney had said he was Korean, and there was no love lost between the South Koreans and the Chinese. So it was extremely doubtful that he'd have had any friends in the Triad. Suddenly he became aware that Casey had been trying to get his attention.

"Sandy... Sandy?"

"Oh, sorry, Case, I was thinking about something."

"Can't blame you. It's been easy to get sidetracked the last day or so."

"It has. So, what were you saying?"

But before Casey could begin, their server appeared, interrupting the conversation. She smiled at them while reciting the daily specials and taking their drink orders. After she'd gone, Casey said, "You know how you and Murph have your outboards laying up against the bulkhead over by the pool? I'm considering putting in perpendicular floating docks for them and adding a couple of extra slips. My thinking is that Bill might not want to return to his old slip when he gets out of the hospital. Bad memories and tourists taking pictures for all the wrong reasons. What do you think?"

"I hadn't thought that far ahead, but I'm glad you are. For that matter, he might not want to move back aboard *My Mahi*. I doubt that

I could sleep in the same bed where my wife was murdered and I was attacked. Fortunately, it looks like *Dorado* will be finished in the next few weeks, and that gives him another option." He paused a second. "And I need to get out of the habit of calling him 'Bill.' He'd hate it if he thought I was being nice to him out of pity."

Casey said, "He'd certainly call you out on it. But I know better than to think it'd be because you were pitying him. It's going to be so important for all of us to treat him like normal because things will be anything but normal when he comes back. That's another reason I want to add more slips to *Casey's Cove* and partly why I hope he'll move over with us. He'd be closer to you, Marlin, and Murph; you guys are his closest friends, and he's going to need to lean on you a lot in the foreseeable future. Plus, he likes hanging out at the *Cove Club,* and he'll only be steps away from it there."

Sandy had a faraway look on his face as he said, "You know the best part about this conversation, Casey? The doctors are saying that he's not yet out of the woods, but we're talking about him coming home because we both know he will. Because we know him better than his doctors ever will."

STEPHANIE ARRIVED at *Mallard Cove* mid-afternoon. She'd done all she could at Wallops, the rest that remained was in the realm of forensics, something best left to experts in that field. She was, by nature, a field investigator. She'd pointed the evidence recovery experts at the barge wreck, giving the forensic scientists even more to do, and they didn't need her in their hair. She'd come to the *Cove* to get a firsthand look at *Oar House* and see what would've been Baloney's field of vision from the wheelhouse.

One of the things that served her well in her job was the ability to envision things as they would have been. After reviewing Rik's video footage numerous times, in her mind, she could see the barge from almost any angle. Now all that was left was to "see" it again, but this time from *Oar House.*

She climbed over the crime scene tape at the railing as she boarded the Chris Craft, then went directly to the wheel to look out through both the forward and side windows. Then she searched the helm pod until she found the switch she was looking for. Flipping it on, she then went to the bow and spotted the light bar on the cabin top. Going back to the helm, she shut off the switch and was startled to hear a voice behind her.

"Excuse me, what are you doing on this boat?"

She turned to find a nicely dressed man with Asian features who had silently boarded and snuck up behind her. Taking her leather badge holder from her pocket, she flipped it open, saying, "FBI. Who are you, and why are you aboard this boat without permission?"

The man seemed startled to hear she was with the FBI.

"I am DaeSeong Han, owner of that yacht," he pointed at *Sandra T*, sitting in her slip across the dock. "I am just making sure that you are not some tourist looking around because of the tragedy."

"Oh, so you're a friend of the late owner and are protecting his property?"

"Uh, unfortunately, I never met him before he died. But I wanted to make sure his property was secure."

"And you thought you had the right to ignore the crime scene tape and trespass like this?"

Han's face reddened, not with embarrassment, but with anger. In his country, no woman would have dared to speak to him in such a manner. Controlling his rage, he said, "I intended to help and believed this to be more important."

"You thought wrong, and if you don't want to be arrested for interfering in an investigation, you'll get back on the dock in the next five seconds."

Han's eyes partially shut as he nodded slightly, then silently turned and left.

Normally Stephanie wouldn't have acted as harshly as she had, but something about the man had set off warning bells in her head. If what he said had been true about why he was there, it was more likely that he'd have yelled from the finger pier instead of ignoring the crime scene tape and sneaking up behind her. This seemed more like the actions of someone who wanted to spy on what she was doing rather than chasing off a voyeur.

Something else she'd noted about Han, he had almost lacked an accent, using perfect English until she'd intentionally upset him. Then his accent and clipped speech had erupted in full force. She mentally filed away this little factoid in her memory.

Resuming the task that she'd come here for, she envisioned the barge through the forward windows and finally through the ones at the side. From this standpoint, unless the docking lights weren't half as bright at night as she thought they were, there would have been no way for Baloney to have missed seeing the lift if it was anywhere outside of the container. The docking lights were mounted high enough to have swept their beams across the entire deck of the barge.

These lights would also have illuminated the men that yelled at him, though they probably would have shielded their eyes from the intensity. The bright beam would have likely been painful, stabbing through the dark night. Then as the boat pulled up alongside, the only light coming from the Chris Craft that could have illuminated the men would probably have been from the cabin, spilling through the windows. Doubtful that it would have been bright enough to make any identification of the men on the barge too easy at any kind of distance.

So, her takeaway from the visit so far was that it was very likely that Baloney would've seen the lift if it was on the barge. It was equally as unlikely that he could've ID'd the men aboard, even if one or both were the man or men who later attacked him. That attack had happened at night, and any light would have come from the attacker or attackers. They certainly would've been careful to have kept it away from their own faces.

Stephanie went into the cabin, first noting that the simple lock on the door had been forced, likely jimmied with a pry bar. Two sets of short stairs led down below, both fore and aft of the salon. The latter ended at the door of the master stateroom, where the two young people had been slaughtered in a likely blitz attack. Again, any light would have likely been minimal and would have been controlled by the attackers to keep their advantage of surprise and confusion.

After completing a tour of the cabin spaces, Stephanie returned to the wheelhouse. From there, she spotted Han walking down the dock with another much taller and beefier Caucasian man, making their way over to the parking lot. Neither man so much as glanced over at *Oar House* as they passed by; they were so engrossed in their conversation.

Finally having found the answers she'd been looking for, Stephanie decided to stop by the *Cove Club* to see if anyone was around before heading home for some well-deserved rest. She retrieved her car and drove over through the electric gates at *Casey's Cove*. From where she parked next to the boathouse, she saw the deck areas around the pool and the outdoor kitchen were deserted. She did hear voices coming from the far side of the boat basin, so she followed them, discovering Casey and Sandy standing by the seawall. As she walked up, she realized it was a design discussion.

Casey was saying, "...and plenty of power at each slip because while we might not need it now, you never know what'll happen in the future."

"Amen to that."

"Oh, hey, Stephanie. I thought you'd still be working," Casey said.

"I am, though I'm about ready to quit for the day. I just came down to get a better look at that Chris."

Sandy asked, "Any news on Baloney?"

"No. I figured you were more on top of that news than me. I'm just trying to catch the guys who did it."

"Guys? Like plural?"

"Might've only been one, but it could also have been two or more, so I go with plural until we know for sure."

"What do you know?"

"Nothing I can tell you, Sandy. Sorry, procedure and all that. I want to make sure we can put them away when we catch 'em. What are you two up to?" She wanted to avoid any further talk about her investigation.

Casey explained his idea about the new slips and about offering one to Baloney for *Dorado*.

Stephanie nodded. "I hope he takes you up on it. I'd be worried if he stayed in that same slip on that same boat when he comes back, even if that's after we catch the killers. There's been so much publicity about it that the crazies are bound to get stirred up. There's no sense in advertising his location. Even if he keeps using *My Mahi* in the show, I hope he'll live here on his new one. It's so much more secure and secluded, as far as his security is concerned. Plus, closer to the rest of the gang. He's going to need us, especially you, Sandy, after he gets out."

Casey said, "Dawn and I were thinking about having him come and stay with us on *Lady Dawn* for a bit, at least until *Dorado* is ready. Then we'll be around him, and so will our crew. Or, he can stay in the pool house guest quarters. Whatever he wants to do. But we'll all stick close to him, no matter what."

"Casey hasn't been over to see the progress on *Dorado*, so we're going to take a field trip over there in my outboard. Want to come along?" Sandy asked.

"Sure. The last time I saw it, the wheelhouse was still smoking." Stephanie had led the group of agents that raided the headquarters of the criminal from Bermuda who had ripped off Murph and Lindsay. She'd arrived as the big Merritt was still smoldering.

"You won't recognize it. Let's go for a boat ride," he said, motioning to his center console.

11

OPTIONS

Sandy idled the boat out through the small inlet of Casey's Cove, which emptied into the Virginia Inside Passage. This narrow part of the waterway was protected by Holly Bluff Island to the southeast and was always flat calm, being less than two hundred yards wide at this point. Once they were out in the passage, Sandy advanced the throttles until the boat reached its fast cruising speed.

As they passed the end of Holly Bluff Island, the passage opened up into the much wider Magothy Bay. *Albury's Boat Works* was only a couple of miles and a few minutes ahead, but the ride out on the water was good for the trio. Having the wind in your face and running through your hair, the dull roar of the outboards, and the sound of the spray shooting out to the side from underneath the hull, the combination was very therapeutic. It was the break they all needed to clear their heads after a tragic couple of days, and no one spoke; all were lost in their own thoughts and enjoying the moment.

Finally, Sandy made the turn to the west into the channel that had been cut through the muddy, shallow marsh that bordered the bay. After several hundred feet, it opened up into a small basin with some floating docks, a ways, and a pair of travel lift piers. They tied up next to *My Mahi*, which was in a slip that backed up against the seawall.

Stephanie said, "If you guys don't mind, I'd like to take a look at the crime scene while we're here. I know it's the county's case, but I still want to familiarize myself with it."

Sandy nodded. "The key is in the top drawer of the tackle center."

"Would it have been there the night they were attacked?" Stephanie asked.

That hit Sandy. "Yeah, they've kept a key in there ever since they bought this boat. Do you think the killer or killers used it to gain entry?"

She nodded. "It's possible. It's a common practice on sportfishing boats with multiple crew members or even mechanics who might need to get in when the captain isn't around."

A tackle center is a group of drawers, usually hidden behind a cabinet door, which holds hooks, sinkers, leader wire, and other pieces of tackle.

Stephanie went aboard the sport fisherman while Casey and Sandy waited on the dock. Sandy didn't want to see the crime scene again, and Casey didn't want to see it at all. And while Stephanie had seen worse over her years with the FBI, none had been connected to a friend before. She looked shaken up after she came back out of the cabin.

She commented, "If all that blood in the salon was Baloney's, it's a miracle that he lived."

"There was even more out here; the deck looked like the floor of a slaughterhouse. He's every bit as tough as he talks," Sandy replied. "Let's go see something better."

Sandy led them up a hinged ramp into the boatyard, then over to the same tall, enclosed shed where Baloney had brought him on Thursday morning. While only a few days ago, it felt more like a million years had passed.

They went in through the side door just as he had with Baloney, only this time; it felt like he was walking into a different shed. Before, Baloney had radiated an excitement that was contagious. He was showing off the biggest symbol of achievement in both his and Betty's lives. Now, with Sandy as the tour guide, this trip was about seeing Baloney's future living options instead of celebrating achievements.

Sandy was amazed at how much progress had been made in only two days. The exterior of the wheelhouse and flybridge had been sprayed with white polyurethane paint, and every inch of *Dorado*'s exterior now looked like the new fishing yacht that she'd been on the day she left Merritt's yard.

"Carlton's craftsmen have really outdone themselves on her," Casey remarked. He hadn't seen the boat since he'd helped Baloney tow it into the yard after the auction. "I'm glad that Baloney also went with white for the hull. She's looking like the classic that she is."

"Wait until you see the interior," Sandy replied. He'd seen that some of the masking paper had been removed in front of the cabin door, allowing access. "He was springing it on Betty as a surprise."

As they went through the doorway into the cabin, Casey and Stephanie were awed at the beautiful woodwork and flawless varnish finishes.

"When I met him only a few years ago, he was barely making a living. To have come this far but to have lost your life partner, I can't imagine how he's going to feel coming home to this by himself," Casey said.

Stephanie nodded. "With what I just saw on *My Mahi*, I can't imagine him living back aboard it. But then again, we're talking about Baloney, who can sometimes be very sentimental and stubborn. In my mind, though, this is the far better option."

"Yeah, and with as far along as this boat is, I'll need to get the new docks in right away. Though *Dorado* will probably be ready to come home before Baloney."

The trio left the shed, heading back to Sandy's boat, when they spotted Han and Eric coming from an area known as "the slab." This is the place where boats that are hauled out with the travel lift are set up "on the hard" for storage and maintenance. Eric saw Sandy and waved.

"Hello, Sandy!" They walked over and met the trio in the middle of the yard.

"Hello, Eric. Fancy meeting you here."

"Just taking a look at Han's…"

Han interrupted, asking rather frostily, "Just what interest does the FBI have here?"

Eric looked surprised. "FBI?"

Stephanie nodded and stuck out her hand, which Eric shook. "Special Agent Stephanie Baker. And you are?"

"Eric Cottell. An acquaintance of Sandy's." He noted that she didn't offer to shake Han's hand, who looked less than happy to see her. Instead, she glared at Han.

"You still did not answer my question. What interest does the FBI have in this boatyard," Han demanded.

"Seeing as I'm off duty, the answer is 'none.' Why do you ask? Is there something here that needs looking into?"

Surprised at how uncomfortable things had become, Eric quickly sought to diffuse things, offering his hand to Casey. "Eric Cottell."

Casey shook the offered hand. "Casey Shaw. Nice to meet you, Eric; I've heard a bit about you."

Han turned to Casey and offered his hand, again snubbing Stephanie. "DaeSeong Han."

This time it was Casey's turn to be curt, opting only to nod instead of taking the offered hand. "Casey Shaw." If Han were going to be a jerk to Stephanie, he'd only get the bare minimum of courtesy from Casey, who trusted her instincts.

Eric saw that this was still going downhill fast and said, "Yes, well, we must be going. Very nice to meet you, Casey, and Stephanie." He and Han resumed their walk toward the parking area.

Once the duo was out of earshot, Stephanie told her friends about her earlier interaction with Han.

"It seems that you made quite an impression on him," Sandy said, chuckling.

"Yeah, well, he had the same effect on me. I wonder what he was doing here?"

Sandy said, "Baloney told me that he had his buyboat refurbished here and replaced the diesel engine with electric. You can imagine how well that set with him." He told Stephanie about having cocktail hour on Eric's boat and explained about Eric's Nonox system and how Baloney was interested in trying it in the *Golden Dolphin*.

"I still wonder what Han was doing here. He pointed out his boat over at Mallard Cove, so it's not back here. And it sounds like your pal Eric wouldn't be very interested in converting to electric power." Stephanie wasn't much of a believer in coincidences, and Han showing up when they were here was suspicious.

Casey suggested, "You know how boatyards have such an attraction for real boaters. Kind of like how baseball fanatics like visiting the different parks. I'm always poking around in new boatyards when I get the chance, just out of curiosity. With those guys, it sounds more like research."

"Maybe." Stephanie didn't sound that convinced. "Han sure cut Eric off from explaining what they were up to. I don't trust Han. There was no real reason for him to show up aboard *Oar House* today. The line he gave me about protecting the boat was total crap."

"I don't know what to tell you. I think the events of the last two days have us all feeling a little off. But it's nothing that one or two of Casey's beers won't help." Sandy grinned.

"You're making me miss Baloney more than ever," Casey said. "But I do have some cold Red Stripes waiting back at the *Cove Club*. Let's go."

~

"The FBI is here."

"Yes, I have already heard. It was to be expected once they determined the cause of the launch failure. They will probably be visiting all the marinas, asking questions about transient boats."

"No. I mean, they are *here* now. One was snooping around that old boat, around the steering wheel where Bigmouth had been."

"Do you think they suspect something?"

"I am not sure, but I do not like them being this close. Though it was only a woman agent. I ran into her again at that boatyard, the one where you had the tug taken out of the water. Bigmouth's boat is being cleaned and repaired there as well."

"That is not good, seeing the FBI twice in one day. It sounds like you could be a suspect."

"I do not know. But I am worried," Han admitted.

"You are smart to be worried and to take precautions. There is a recovery vessel now anchored over the barge wreck. They have been diving on it all day, bringing up small pieces of the lift."

"What! How could they have found it, and so fast? Why are they looking at it?"

"I do not know, but they must suspect something."

"All that should be left of it is small pieces. The device was powerful."

"You should leave there immediately. And make sure you are seen leaving but that it does not look like you are panicked; it should seem like this was planned in advance. Do not let the FBI think that you are running; you should appear relaxed. Then come here; my men will be waiting to remove your cargo mast. We will fit you under the covered shed where any planes or drones cannot spot your boat." He paused. "Tonight, we will remove the last piece that could connect you with the barge."

"Bigmouth?"

"No. He must have already told them about the barge; otherwise, how could they have known about it? If he had seen you or your boat, he would have told them about that, too, and you would already have been arrested."

"After we were hit, I hid inside the container in the dark. There is no way that he saw me, only your two men."

"That is bad enough."

Eric spotted Han backing out of his slip. As he passed *Providence*, Han stuck his arm out of the wheelhouse and gave a friendly wave, which Eric returned. He assumed Han was going for a sunset cruise out in the bay.

It wasn't until an hour later, when he walked up to the *Cove* for dinner, that he noticed Han had taken his dock box, hose, and shore power cord with him. Something he wouldn't have done if he was only going for a short cruise or even for an overnight trip. He must be relocating, but he hadn't mentioned this. In fact, they were supposed to keep working on a deal for an emulsion device installation for Han's small tugboat, which was located over at *Albury's Boat Works*.

Eric called Han's cell phone, only to find that it had been disconnected. He sighed, thinking *buyers are liars.* Han wasn't the first to renege on a deal with him, and the truth was, he should've seen this coming. After all, the man had spent a small fortune converting his buyboat to electric power.

The small diesel tugboat hadn't seemed to fit his style. Han didn't mention having any kind of marine business, and the tug appeared to have already been winterized, though cold weather was many months away. *What an odd little man*, Eric thought as he continued down the dock to the restaurant.

A little before 3:00 a.m., Monday morning...

The black inflatable with its four-stroke outboard idled quietly into *Mallard Cove's* basin. The two men aboard it were dressed in dark clothing, with long sleeves covering the Triad tattoos on their forearms. Without a word, the man in the bow stepped over onto the finger pier, heaving a short tow line onto the bow of the old Chris Craft. As he walked toward the stern of the boat, he didn't bother untying its dock lines, opting instead to sever each one with his razor-sharp tactical knife. Then he disconnected the shore power cord from the dock's power pedestal and tossed it aboard.

Carrying a small plastic container, he climbed aboard the now free-floating boat, hurrying to the bow and attaching the tow line to a cleat. Then he gave his accomplice a silent wave, which was barely visible against the glow of the dim dock lights behind him. The small inflatable began slowly towing the much larger boat out of its slip and over toward the basin's inlet.

Even without adding a lot of throttle, the momentum of the larger boat began to build as it followed along behind its smaller tow boat. With the engine barely above idle, the only sound the man on the bow of the Chris Craft could hear was the sound of the water stream of the outboard engine's telltale indicator. This was more commonly referred to around the docks as the pee hole, as it sounded like someone relieving themselves into the water. It wasn't likely to wake anyone sleeping aboard any of the other boats.

Fortunately, this summer morning was completely still, and the larger boat fell perfectly in line behind the outboard as they went out through the inlet. Once they were about fifty yards beyond the mouth, the man in the inflatable gave his engine some gas, speeding up the process. Without running lights, the two boats had disappeared into the pitch-black, moonless night. From shore, their silhouettes could barely be seen against the orange glow of the streetlights in Virginia Beach, about fifteen miles distant.

After they were a quarter mile out, near Fisherman Island in Smith Island Inlet, the man in the outboard slowed the engine before finally switching into neutral. His accomplice came back up onto the bow, uncleating the tow line and tossing it into the outboard.

He'd been busy during the tow, preparing the boat for what was to come next. As he went back aft to the open boarding area of the railing, he could smell the gasoline that he'd spread around the salon and out onto the aft deck. He lit a cigarette and placed it inside the hinge of a pack of matches before closing it. Placing it carefully next to a small puddle of gas, he quickly dropped down into the inflatable as his partner accelerated away from the old boat.

They were almost a mile away when the cigarette ignited all of the match heads, lighting the gas at the same time. It was completely engulfed by the time an early-rising motorist spotted the fire from the bridge of the Chesapeake Bay Bridge-Tunnel and reported it to the Coast Guard. By the time a boat from the Cape Charles station arrived, the boat had almost burned down to the waterline. What was left soon sank, though it didn't have far to go. They had inadvertently left it floating with its bottom only a foot above a sandbar, making the removal of what was left, as well as the investigation into the cause, that much easier.

12

THE MESSAGE

M *onday, 7:00 A.M.*

"HELLO?" While it didn't wake her, Stephanie knew that an early morning phone call like this one usually signaled a long work day ahead. It was Casey Shaw on the line.

"Hey, Stephanie. We've got an interesting morning going at *Mallard Cove*. Last night, someone stole *Oar House* and set it on fire next to Fisherman Island. What's left of it sunk in the shallows."

"Well, that's more of a morning bracer than a second cup of coffee. It sounds like someone is tying up some loose ends."

"That's my guess as well. Though it's interesting, our sheriff isn't the least bit interested in investigating it further other than taking a report like you'd need for an insurance claim. He says it's a Coast Guard matter, even though it was stolen from *Mallard Cove*."

"Funny how things like that happen in their office. Have you told Rik?"

"She's on my list to call next."

Stephanie took a moment to think before continuing. "It doesn't make a lot of sense. The crime scene techs had already completely processed the boat. There shouldn't have been anything left that the killer needed to hide."

"Somebody thought there was. So did you, enough to visit the scene yesterday."

"True, though that was just a visual sightline thing. Might've made somebody nervous, though. This reminds me, I think I'll have a little chat with our pal Han this morning."

"That could prove to be a bit difficult. He pulled out of here yesterday, a little before sundown. Angel over at the *Beach Bar* saw his boat headed west toward the Fisherman Inlet Bridge. She's working at the *Cove* on the deck this morning if you want to talk to her."

"I might, thanks. So then, a few hours after I was aboard *Oar House*, she gets destroyed. How convenient. I don't suppose anyone saw who stole it?"

"It must have happened around two or three, not exactly a busy time in the marina on a Monday morning, so that's a 'no.'"

"Well, if Bromwell's office won't investigate this, I will. I'll head your way in a few minutes."

"I'll be gone for a bit; Sandy and I are going to the hospital to check on Baloney. Probably be there for a couple of hours."

"No problem, Casey. I'll see you when I see you."

THE FOG WASN'T AS THICK, and Baloney could hear much of what was going on around him. There was no sign of that boat or anyone with an Asian accent, though. He listened harder and was certain he recognized the two male voices that were talking with a female voice.

THE NURSE WAS TELLING them that they started weaning Bill off the sedation overnight and expected him to be somewhat awake by the afternoon, though he'd be groggy since he will still be on strong painkillers. She said that if all goes well, he'll be moved out of SICU later today and into a regular room.

"Case... Hack."

Hearing his voice startled the nurse, who then quickly checked Baloney, who still hadn't opened his eyes. "Captain Cooper, don't try to talk right now. You need your save your strength so you can heal."

"I... need... a beer."

Sandy grinned and leaned in close to his ear, saying, "Welcome back, Gilligan."

CASEY AND SANDY were sitting in the waiting room when Debbie walked in. She saw they looked much happier than they had before. Sandy quickly brought her up to date on his condition, and she was so relieved. Then he saw her face tighten.

"What is it?" he asked.

"We'll have to tell him about Aunt Betty. I guess I should be the one to do it."

"Wait and play it by ear, Debbie. He's making much better progress than they'd hoped for. We don't want to set back his recovery."

She nodded. "I'll wait until he asks."

"Good plan."

WHEN DEBBIE and Sandy went in at the top of the hour, they found him much more alert, with his eyes partially open. Debbie took his hand and smiled at him.

"Hi, Uncle Bill."

He squeezed her hand slightly and started to say something when Sandy interrupted him, "They said you shouldn't talk, Gilligan."

"Screw... them... Hack."

"Uncle Bill! Do like they say so that you can come home soon."

Baloney's eyes focused on her for a second; then he nodded slightly as he closed them, but he still held onto her hand.

"When you come home, I'll personally bring you a case of Kalik. Pre-chilled," Sandy said, as Baloney smiled slightly.

～

STEPHANIE WENT STRAIGHT to the now-empty slip that had been occupied by *Oar House*. Surprisingly, the parts of the dock lines that had been left behind were still attached to the cleats. Though maybe she shouldn't be surprised, she thought, since Bromwell was taking a pass on this investigation.

She went to her car and grabbed gloves and evidence bags, then went back and collected the rope remnants. It was a long shot that they might contain some touch DNA, or that the cuts might be able to be matched to a specific knife or type of knife. But that couldn't happen without the lines being collected first, she thought. Investigating the Northampton SO was definitely going to be discussed in her office.

Her next stop was at the empty slip where the *Sandra T* had been docked. Not surprisingly, nothing had been left behind on the dock. The trash can had also been emptied, with a new liner in place. Also, not surprising since *Mallard Cove* was so well run.

Stephanie went to *Providence* next, knocking on the hull to get Eric's attention. When he came out of the salon, he instantly recognized her.

"Well, hello! What can I do for the FBI today?"

"I have a few questions for you, if you don't mind."

"Not at all. Would you like to come inside and chat? I just made a fresh pot of coffee if you'd like some."

She started up the gangway. "I'll take you up on that." She took a seat in the air-conditioned salon while Eric brought up two cups from the galley.

"I'd like to talk to you about your friend, Han."

"He's more of an acquaintance, really, and definitely not a friend. I thought he was going to be a customer until he pulled a vanishing act last night. I'm kind of glad he did."

"Wait, I thought his boat had recently been converted to electric drive. How was he going to be a customer?"

"The one that he had here is electric. I'm talking about the tugboat that he has up on the hard at Albury's boatyard."

"What tugboat? I wasn't aware he had more than the buyboat."

"It's a small one with an eight-cylinder diesel. Big enough to push a small work barge, but anything much over seventy or eighty feet, and you'd probably have your hands full trying to steer it." He paused, cocking his head slightly as he thought. "It's funny, you know; he didn't seem the type to be involved in light marine transport or construction, and that's what that old tug looked to be best suited for. With the way that he dressed and acted, that teak-decked buyboat seemed to fit him much better."

"Did he tell you where he was going?"

"No, I don't have a clue. I didn't even know he was leaving. But, as I said, I'm glad he's gone. Last night, I began thinking back to some of what he told me. I know now that he was interested in my emulsion fuel system mostly for fuel savings, not pollution reduction. He said his country had sanction restrictions on how much fuel it was allowed to import and that they have almost no oil production of their own."

He stopped and sipped his coffee, watching to see if Stephanie might already know where he was headed with this. All he saw was her best poker face. Then he continued.

"When I came back to the boat, I looked up online about Korea's oil sanctions. There are no restrictions on South Korea's oil imports, and they have a growing domestic hydrocarbon production industry, both on land and offshore. But North Korea has sanctions in place on it that limits imports, and while it appears they might have decent reserves in the ground and under the sea, they produce less than two hundred barrels per day while using over twenty thousand.

"So, he wasn't really interested in my system for that tug. I'm certain now that he was going to steal the technology and take it back to North Korea, which must be his real home, the bloody snake! They're constantly smuggling illegal oil in excess of what they are allowed. My system could mean up to the equivalent of a fifteen-percent increase in that allowance under those sanctions."

Now it was all making sense to Stephanie as all of the other pieces of the puzzle began dropping into place.

"Eric, I need you to keep all of what you just told me in confidence. Are you planning on leaving anytime soon?"

"Probably not for another two weeks or so."

"Good. There will be some people from another government agency that will want to talk to you about Han."

"You're thinking this all is related to the murders and the attack on that Baloney character." It was both a statement as well as a question.

Stephanie nodded. "Which is part of why I need you to keep this all confidential."

"Don't give it another thought. If Han's responsible for those attacks, I'd love to see you capture him before I go back to the Bahamas. Baloney is more than a bit strange, but he grows on you and certainly didn't deserve what happened to him and his wife. I'll be happy to do whatever I can to help."

LATE IN THE AFTERNOON, Baloney was transferred into a private room. It looked more like a parade than a transfer, as he was followed closely by his four bodyguards, along with Debbie, Sandy, and Casey. Fortunately, the new room came with new, more lax visitation rules. The hours ran from 9:00 a.m. to 9:00 p.m., and up to four people at a time could visit, over and above his security detail.

Baloney had made great progress during the day, becoming more and more alert, aware, and able to talk. Though he tended to drift off quickly after each time that he pushed the boost button on his morphine drip.

Detective Aldrich came by an hour after Baloney was moved. Sandy spotted him in the hall and headed him off.

"We haven't told Bill about Betty and the others yet. We're waiting until he asks or is stronger. Don't wear him out; he tires easily."

"You just stick to writing books and don't try to tell me how to do my job. I've got a killer to catch, and I'm not lettin' anybody stand in my way, Morgan." He shoved past Sandy and went into the room.

"I'm Detective Aldrich, Captain Cooper. What do you remember of your attack?" He glanced at Sandy, silently making the point that he'd kept his question only about Baloney.

"Nothin'. I was on that ol' Chris, an' then I woke up here." The sentence took all his effort.

"Do you remember if it was one attacker or two?"

Baloney shook his head gently. "Nah. Nuthin'."

"Did he or they say anything?"

"Don't remember."

Clearly disappointed, Aldrich said, "I may be back when I have more questions."

Baloney nodded. "Okay." He closed his eyes and appeared to be asleep instantly.

Aldrich glared at Sandy silently as he passed him on his way out. Sandy returned the look.

"You kids don't much like each other," Casey noted.

"I don't think there's a lot to like in that one. Dumb son of a bitch with a badge, and that's a bad combination. Almost ended up with me in jail because he's so stubborn and stupid."

"You're right; that is a bad combination."

By the last hour of allowable visitation, the ones that were left in the room were Sandy, Debbie, and two security guys. Rikki had decreased the number in the detail because they were able to be in the room with Baloney rather than in the hall, out of direct sight.

Baloney had been sleeping, but now he opened his eyes and said, "Debbie?"

She stepped closer to the bed. "Right here, Uncle Bill."

"Don't worry... I know about Betty."

Shocked, she asked, "Wait, who told you?"

"She did... When I died... It's okay... She's okay."

Debbie looked over at Sandy, who was just as shocked as she was. She turned back to Baloney and said, "But you didn't die, Uncle Bill. You're here with us."

"Died twice. Got sent back. She'll be there when it's really my turn. That last sentence sounded a bit fuzzy as he'd hit the boost button on the morphine again. He closed his eyes and began to snore very lightly, sounding almost like a purr.

~

MARLIN SAW the headlights of Sandy's truck as he pulled into *Casey's Cove*. He hurried out of his house barge, intercepting him as he was about to reach his floating finger pier.

"Hey Sandy, how's Baloney?"

"Doing better than they thought he would and getting better faster. They moved him into a private room."

"Oh good, I was waiting to visit until they did that. I mean, if it would be a good idea..."

Sandy cut him off. "Good idea? I think if you don't go soon, you'll get an earful when you see him next."

"I bet he's tired."

"*He's* tired? I'm *exhausted*! Been a hell of a few days. I need a beer, my cat, some food, and about a hundred hours of sleep. You want a beer?"

"I can run and get us some off my houseboat."

"Don't worry about it; we'll drink mine."

"Now I know you're tired when you start giving away beer, Sandy."

"Funny guy. Hey, KC, I was just talking about you." The cat came racing down the gangway and over to Sandy, rubbing on his calf. "I bet you're hungry."

"Looks more like he missed you than anything else."

The trio started down the finger pier and up the gangway.

"Don't kid yourself, Marlin; he knows what's going on. If it hadn't been for him, we'd have lost Baloney as well. Cats know things. They have a sense that we don't, and that's why he knew Bill was in trouble."

Sandy fed KC and pulled two bottles of beer from the refrigerator. Marlin settled into an armchair while Sandy plopped onto the sofa, putting his feet up on an ottoman.

Sandy said, "Speaking of knowing things, Bill knows about Betty."

Marlin grimaced. "That must've been tough to tell him."

"That's just it; none of us did. He said Betty told him when he died."

"He said *what* when he did *what*?"

Sandy took a long sip of beer and then continued, "He said he saw her and that he died twice." He looked straight into Marlin's eyes. "Thing about it is, his heart stopped twice, and they brought him back both times. Marlin, Bill was so at peace when he told Debbie and me about seeing Betty and being told she was gone. How else could he have known? It was total acceptance without grief. I've never seen anything like it before."

"I was worried about going, I didn't know if he'd been told about Betty and how he would handle it if he had been."

"After he told me, it took some of my own grief away. I think it's the closest thing I've seen to true peace, and it's like it is contagious. So, don't worry, just go."

"I will tomorrow morning."

"Has the show been getting a lot of emails about him?"

"You have no idea. Emails, calls, you name it. Fans have been sending flowers to the office since he couldn't have them in ICU. If you think he was popular before, now he's off the charts."

Sandy rolled his eyes as he said, "There's going to be no living with him, but at least he'll still be living with us."

Marlin raised his bottle in a salute. "Here's to that."

13

BOAT FOR SALE

T*en days later...*

"I APPRECIATE YA PUTTIN' me up for a few days. I'll be outta yer hair just as soon as Carlton gets *Dorado* finished," Baloney said.

Casey, Dawn, and Sandy were bringing him back to *Lady Dawn*. They had gotten Baloney to see the logic in having people around him all the time as he recuperated. It would be a couple of weeks more until he was fully mobile and off any pain medications. Except for beer, of course, despite his doctor's warning against mixing the two.

Dawn said, "You don't need to be in any hurry to rush off. Our crew gets tired of only having Casey and me aboard. They like it when we have company; it helps eliminate the boredom of doing the same thing every day."

"Company... more like a burden, ya mean, but thanks. Glad ta have friends like you guys. Even you, Hack." He grinned at Sandy.

"I'd love to tell you how much you've been missed, Gilligan. I can say that because I only write fiction."

"Speakin' ah that, when're ya gonna get back to it?"

"Soon, soon. Let's get you back to normal first. Whatever that is."

Baloney nodded and looked away. He'd been doing this a lot lately. Sandy suspected that despite his original belief about Betty telling him she'd be waiting for him when it was his turn to go, this was part of his grieving process.

ONCE BALONEY WAS safe aboard *Lady Dawn*, Andrea O'Neil was put in charge of looking after him. Baloney was now sitting with Dawn, Casey, and Sandy on the covered aft deck, looking across the cove's jetty toward the Inside Passage. Andrea came up beside him.

"Anything you need, Captain Cooper, I'll be glad to take care of for you," she said.

"The first thing ya can do for me is call me Baloney like everybody else does. But I'm good for now, thanks." He looked around, enjoying sitting outdoors for the first time in almost two weeks. Rikki's protection team was now gone since Baloney was safely back within the secure confines of *Casey's Cove*. Plus, *Lady Dawn* had video cameras and infrared motion detectors that monitored anyone who approached the yacht. Most of the crew, along with Casey and Dawn, all carried concealed weapons and were well-trained in their use. There was almost no safer place for Baloney to be.

"Well, Bill, it's about time you got back to work! I've had to hire another person in the publicity department to handle all your added fan mail," Marlin said as he walked out of the salon with Debbie. Both were carrying boxes filled with cards and letters from concerned fans.

"Ya mean Debbie? I was gonna talk to you about maybe hirin' her."

"Marlin approached me at the hospital. I thought you had talked to him about me already. You hadn't?" Debbie turned to Marlin, who shook his head.

"Nope, he didn't need to ask me to hire you; I saw that you were dedicated and organized, with the way that you took charge of his care. I figured you'd bring those same attributes to work on the show, and I was right. Now you're still in charge of him, but the first task is about getting all of these answered. I've got folks in the office that have been working on all the emails that've been piling up."

"Wait, I gotta answer all ah *those*? There's gotta be a thousand of 'em," Baloney exclaimed.

Debbie grinned. "At least. And yes, we're going to answer each and every one of them. If they took the time and went to the extra effort of writing you, the least you can do is hand write them back. These folks are all worried about you. And it's not like you're going to go back to charter fishing anytime soon."

"Yeah. Maybe not ever. I been thinkin' about that. I'm gonna move Bobby over to *My Mahi* an' get somebody else ta run the *Golden Dolphin*. I'll still do the show with Bobby on *Mahi*, but then I'm free ta do other shows th' rest of th' year.

"Speakin' ah that, I got this idea, Marlin. What would ya think about a show where the Hack an' me go fishin' all over th' place? Back ta the Keys, fishin' with some ah his old friends, mebbe down ta Costa Rica, th' Bahamas an' all over. Ah course, he buys the beer wherever we end up."

"Huh? Wait a minute, when were you going to talk to me about this idea, Gilligan," Sandy questioned.

"Thought I just did, Hack. Whatcha think about it, Marlin?"

"I think it would be pure ratings gold. That is if Sandy is interested."

"Hell no, I'm not interested. Not unless Gilligan buys the beer!"

Marlin held up a hand, "We'll let the show buy the beer."

"No! He buys it," Baloney and Sandy said simultaneously, pointing at each other.

Marlin grinned. "Make that pure ratings *platinum*."

Dawn asked, "What about your writing, Sandy?"

"That's what laptops are for. And I know a guy from Virginia Beach that sells small portable satellite internet uplinks. With one of those, I could work from anywhere."

A few minutes later, Casey and Sandy walked into the salon,

leaving the others talking together outside. Casey said, "I'm surprised that you agreed to do the show, especially how quickly you made your decision."

"It was a 'no-brainer,' Case. It wasn't about the show, although I have to hand it to Gilligan; it does sound like fun. It's more about me being there for him. I know he says he's fine because Betty supposedly told him from the 'great beyond' that she was good, but I'm not fully buying it. At some point, it's going to hit him like a brick wall falling over on him, and I intend on being there when it does.

"Don't forget, I lost my wife, too. Though it was cancer that took her life, not some intruder. It's been a few years now, but I still get things that pop into my head that I'll think I need to tell her until I remember that I can't. It hurts less and less as the years go by, but it still hurts.

"I think this new show idea will be a great thing to keep his mind occupied, especially if we're traveling around and he's not having to look at *My Mahi* every day. Kind of like therapy that pays you instead of the other way around."

Casey smiled. "When you two first met, I thought you were going to end up coming to blows. He's got a lot of friends, Sandy, but none better than you turned out to be."

"I don't know about that, Case. Putting him up here, adding the new slip, I'd say you're a damn good friend."

"Talk about timing; here comes Jack Miller now." Casey pointed out the window at a barge with a crane aboard that was coming through the inlet into the basin. Jack Miller had built all of the docks for the Shaw properties. "I guess I should go talk to Baloney about this."

"Probably a good idea," Sandy said as he rolled his eyes. "You and he kind of procrastinate over sharing your ideas."

The pair walked back out to the aft deck, and Baloney asked Casey, "What's Jack Miller doin' here?"

"Well, Bill, we got to thinking..."

Baloney interrupted him, "*Bill?* This is gonna be bad."

"Hear him out, Gilligan," Sandy insisted.

Baloney scowled. "Yer in on it, too? I shoulda known."

"Will you shut up and listen to the man? But yes, we're all 'in on it.' Though it doesn't mean you have to do it," Sandy said. "Tell him, Casey."

"As I was saying, we were all thinking that people are going to be bothering you twenty-four-seven for the foreseeable future. And *My Mahi* is a big part of your brand, so I know you'll still want her over there where she can be seen from the restaurant. But you aren't likely to find any peace and quiet around her.

"I didn't like having the outboards getting beaten up laying against the bulkhead when storms come through, so I decided to add some floating dock slips over there that run perpendicular to the seawall, not parallel. And there was room to add a couple of extra slips because of this. We were all thinking that if you were still going to move aboard *Dorado*, this might be a good place for her."

Baloney looked at the faces of his friends and his niece. Faces filled with concern. He weighed his options, but only for a few seconds.

"Yeah, I'm still movin' onta her when she's ready. Can I have th' slip that's closest ta th' pool?"

Sandy said, "You mean closest to Casey's beer fridge in the outdoor kitchen!"

"Well, yeah, that too."

Everyone laughed, even Baloney. Casey said, "Whichever slip that you would like."

"That'd be great, thanks Case an' Dawn. But about *Mahi*. I been thinkin', an' I'm puttin' that one up for sale. I can't go back aboard her. An' Pete Jones has a new fifty-three-footer he's buildin' that's for sale. A real beaut, and it's almost done. Built from th' get-go as a charter boat, ya know? Interior ya can spray down with a hose if ya want, all fiberglass an' paint. Comfortable but not fancy. A real fisherman's fishin' boat. Gonna have it painted the same hull color as *Mahi*, but I'm gonna call it *Bull Dolphin*."

A bull dolphin is a larger male mahi, which has a distinctive, square forehead.

"Sounds like a great plan, Baloney," Marlin said as Dawn reached over and put a hand on Baloney's shoulder, silently agreeing while not daring to try and speak. Between raging pregnancy hormones and the loss of Betty, this would have made it too difficult to say anything, and she knew that she'd have lost it. When Baloney reached up and patted her hand, the tears still began streaming down her face.

"Aw, Dawn, don't be doin' that. Ya know Betty woulda been upset ta see ya sad. She always said you have the best smile."

Baloney had no sooner finished saying that when there was a loud metallic rumble from across the basin as Jack Miller's crew dropped the barge's large pipe spuds. These are two large pointed pipes that slide down through tubes in the barge's hull and stick in the bottom, anchoring it in place. Then the crane cranked up and began raising the diesel pile driver, getting ready to install the first of the large metal pilings that would anchor the new floating docks.

"Yeah, well, that's enough fresh air for me for a while. My ears are about the only things th' docs didn't hafta work on, and I wanna keep it that way. Time ta get inside before that noisy mother cranks up. Somebody gimme a hand up outta this chair."

FONG WENT over into the covered boat shed, feeling the summer heat that was radiating from the corrugated metal roof. The *Sandra T* was floating in her slip, motionless and silent except for the air conditioner's cooling water pouring from a thru-hull fitting in her side. He knocked on the hull, and Han opened the wheelhouse door.

"Come aboard into the air-conditioning. It is much too hot to be outside the cabin while we are in this shed."

Fong climbed aboard and went into the wheelhouse, which contained a built-in bunk aft, and two chairs anchored with stanchions, each facing forward out through the windows. Han indicated one of the chairs as he slipped into the other and swiveled to face Fong.

"It is not good news," Fong said. "My law enforcement contacts tell me that instead of losing interest, the FBI has increased their efforts to find you and are calling you 'a primary person of interest' in the attacks at *Mallard Cove Marina*."

Han exploded. "Yet you and your men carried out the attacks; I merely paid you. So, now my men and I are stuck in this infernal oven, unable to be seen outside for fear of arrest, all because your men failed to post anchor lights on that damned barge!

"Ten days stuck aboard is more than I can stand. I need to get out of here, even if I have to take this boat out at night so I can once again stand on the deck and breathe fresh air."

Fong said gently, as not to further enflame things, "They are circulating pictures of your boat, as well as a picture of you that some tourist took when you and Bigmouth were arguing. Apparently, he is some kind of celebrity."

Han grunted. "One that is harder to kill than he appeared."

"Yes. But I have somewhat of a solution for you and your men. You will be my guest at my house for dinner, and your men can eat with my men in the kitchen in the warehouse. Wait until after it gets dark, say at nine fifteen, and move quickly in case there are any drones overhead." Fong was playing to Han's paranoia, which had been increasing by the day.

"Of course, and I am honored to be invited to your home, and I will make sure that my men are in the warehouse on time." He bowed slightly to Fong, who matched it.

FONG WENT from the boat shed over to the warehouse and into a back room that also served as a small workshop. There one of his men was busy grinding off the last remnants of a barb on a stainless-steel speargun shaft. The man was an expert with both mechanical and electronic devices.

"Is the tip sharp enough?" Fong asked.

His man said, "I ground it down further to improve the angle and make it less blunt. Then I filed that section until it was smooth. I was just about to test it."

The two went out into the warehouse where a range of sorts had been created. The backstop was a Styrofoam archery target with ten layers of corrugated cardboard sandwiched together and attached in front of it.

The man said, "The tip is going to be within a meter of the box, so I am replicating the distance exactly to see if the spear has enough velocity to penetrate all the layers of cardboard. This should be much stronger than the plastic sides but also take into account the resistance it will have as it comes into contact with the individual cells themselves."

"You're sure this will work?" Fong asked.

"We will know shortly." The speargun itself was slightly longer than a meter, and the man put the butt of the gun on the floor. He carefully slipped a loading device consisting of a form-fitting metal cap with a finger hold on either side over the tip of the spear. He then placed the blunt end of the shaft into the barrel and pulled down on the loader until all but a few inches of the shaft disappeared into the gun. Removing the loader, he selected the high-power setting, giving the spear the most velocity possible.

Aiming at the target from three feet away, he pulled the trigger. Both men were surprised to see the spear not only pierce the multiple cardboard layers but pass through the Styrofoam and stick out several inches beyond the back.

"Excellent," Fong said. "You are certain this will cause the reaction that we want?"

"Absolutely. You will get exactly the result you desire."

"What about the trigger mechanism?"

The man led Fong back into the small shop. Picking up a pincer device from the workbench, he said, "This will be attached to the trigger on the speargun. An optical sensor activates a timer once it senses the movement of the propeller shaft. The delay can be set between one minute and one hour. Then it energizes the pincer, squeezing the trigger on the speargun, firing it. Simple and effective."

Fong said, "Set it for thirty-five minutes. This should give them just enough time to reach the tip of the Eastern Shore, making it seem that perhaps they were returning to the crime scene for something and leading the FBI away from here. Very good work."

"Thank you, sir."

"Wait until you see Han's men go into the kitchen, then five minutes later, take this equipment and install it on the boat. At 9:55, they will be racing back to their boat and leaving, so you will need to be finished and gone by then."

"It will be done."

HAN APPEARED at Fong's front door at exactly 9:15. The house was on the adjoining property, only a two-minute walk from the boat shed.

Fong's house manager opened the door and invited Han in as Fong walked into the foyer. Han removed his shoes as was customary and then followed Fong into a sitting room. The house manager quickly poured and then served each man a drink in fine crystal highball glasses.

"A very rare whiskey from Kentucky. It is the proprietor's own reserve and impossible to find," Fong stated proudly. "To success!" He raised his glass slightly.

Han matched the gesture, then took a sip of the smooth, amber liquid. "Most excellent! The finest whiskey I have ever tasted."

Fong didn't doubt the man's words since he was sure Han wouldn't have had access to anything like this in North Korea, and his contacts here in the States were very limited. Fong, on the other hand, was as connected in the US as he was back in China. This was the reason he'd been contacted by his friends in the Chinese government and asked to act as support for Han's mission. For a price, of course.

"I am glad you approve. One of the benefits of success in this country is being able to afford such luxuries." Fong knew that *Sandra T* and all its modifications were not paid for nor owned by Han but by the government of North Korea. Han was merely a cog in the communist government machine that had assigned him to play the part of a wealthy businessman as his cover.

Han wore a sly smile. "Which I will soon be able to enjoy myself."

This caught Fong by surprise. "Really? I thought you would be going back to your homeland to return to your usual position."

"That is what they believe will happen, but I have stumbled onto something that will make me rich and allow me to remain in this country. There is a device that will stretch my country's fuel supply by up to fifteen percent. This is something that will be almost invaluable to the Supreme Leader, though I have determined my own price." The sly smile now morphed into a smug grin.

Seeing Han's glass was already empty, Fong motioned for his house manager to attend to it. Once his glass was refilled, Han took a long swig of the smooth liquor. Fong wanted to encourage his consumption since he needed to hear more about the device.

Once again, Fong raised his glass. "To your upcoming prosperity, my friend!" He pretended to take a large sip from his glass, wanting to stay sober so that he might pry all the information out of Han that he could right now since the man had just over an hour left to live.

"How did you come across this device?"

Han chuckled. "One of life's ironies. Bigmouth was bragging about his friend having invented it. I approached the man, claiming to be the owner of your tugboat. We inspected it in the boatyard, and he said he would design a device to fit the needs of that engine. We were in the middle of price negotiations when the FBI became involved, and I had to flee." He took another healthy swig of whiskey.

"So, this inventor has undoubtedly heard that you are now wanted and will have stopped all work on the design. You have nothing to trade with your government."

Han snorted and raised his glass for the house manager to refill it. "I don't need the new unit. Eric Cottell, the inventor, has two of the units installed on his Hatteras yacht that is docked at *Mallard Cove*. Since I cannot go back there, my new partner is going to steal the boat, *Providence*, and dispose of anyone on board. Then I will sell one of the two units to my country."

"Who is this new partner?"

"You, of course. You have the men who are capable of performing such a task, and I have the contacts with which to sell the unit. We are perfect to work together." Again, he raised his glass to Fong, who reciprocated.

Only Fong wasn't toasting a new partnership; he was taking in all of what Han had just said. The fool admitted that he had claimed the ownership of the tugboat, which undoubtedly the FBI would eventually connect with the barge. And he underestimated Fong's connections. He didn't need Han to sell the device to North Korea. And he never, ever, took in partners. At least not any that lived very long.

14

THE LAST SUPPER

Fong and Han had moved into the dining room and were into the second of many courses of Chinese delicacies when Fong's phone rang.

"Yes? When? Right." He hung up and looked wide-eyed at Han. "The FBI is on their way here to raid us! You must take your boat and go now!"

But Han was still more than slightly inebriated. The sudden shock and adrenaline were starting to take the edge off of his buzz, though, as he began panicking. "What! Where do I go?"

"Take to the ocean, and set a course for North Carolina. Go to Ocracoke Island if you can. It is very remote, with only one deputy living there, and is highly doubtful that he has heard of you. Go now, I will stall the FBI."

Han went tearing out of Fong's house and over to the warehouse to collect his men. The trio raced over to the boat shed, boarding the *Sandra T* and getting immediately underway. Once out in the Chesapeake, Han set a course for the mouth of the bay, hugging the shoreline.

He shut off all the electrical devices he could to conserve energy to extend their range. This included the air-conditioning and even the radar since he was using a GPS plotter to navigate. Unfortunately for Han, the plotter didn't show all the latest pound net locations. Within sight of the lights on Fisherman Inlet Bridge at the tip of the Eastern Shore, he ran into one of the nets. The bow of his boat snapped off one of the pilings, and the net itself began to wrap around the propeller. The boat lurched to a stop within a couple of its own lengths as the top of the wooden piling became jammed between the propeller and the boat hull, with the net dragging along behind it. The netting on the far side caught the bow and stretched taught between two of the piles. The buyboat coasted into it like someone running into the middle of the net on a tennis court.

At that moment, the speargun fired. As Fong's man had predicted, it easily penetrated the side of the huge battery. He was also correct about its ability to pierce many of the individual lithium-ion battery cells that made up its interior. This caused a thermal runaway within the plastic casing, and the resulting exothermic reaction instantly began producing large quantities of combustible and toxic gases.

As the battery became more and more unstable, the sparks created by the stainless-steel spear contacting several of the individual cell's leads now ignited the gases, combining with the lithium to create a huge fiery explosion. This ripped off most of the deck of the *Sandra T* as it also shattered her wheelhouse, sending body parts and pieces of wood into the air and then raining back down to the surface of the water.

Two miles behind and slightly offshore from her, the crew aboard the twin outboard rigid-hulled inflatable boat (RHIB) from Coast Guard Station Cape Charles observed the explosion. They had been acting on an anonymous phone tip about Han making a run for it. The RHIB had been within a few minutes of catching up to the buyboat, which they had been observing on their radar. The young coastguardsman at the helm told his crew to stand by to recover any survivors, though he doubted there would be any.

The Cove Restaurant deck, *early the next day...*

Sandy was on his second cup of coffee after finishing breakfast. He watched as Stephanie was being dropped off in *My Mahi*'s slip by a small Coast Guard inflatable boat. Looking up, she spotted him and turned toward the steps leading up to the deck. As she approached his table, he said, "Hi Stephanie, had breakfast yet?"

"About four cups of coffee, but nothing solid. Would you mind ordering me a Cove Breakfast Sandwich and an orange juice? I'll be right back."

"Sure... where are you going?"

"Did you miss the part about four cups of coffee?"

Sandy laughed. "Oh, right."

After she returned from the restroom, Sandy asked, "What was up with you and the Coasties this early?"

"I got called out to meet them here a little after midnight. Han's buyboat exploded over past the bridge. When they ID'd the wreck, my contact information was on the BOLO we issued, naming Han as a person of interest and saying that he might be aboard that boat. His was the last body we recovered about an hour ago. Lucky for us, most of the debris and the bodies got trapped in a pound net they'd hit."

"Damn," Sandy swore. "Taking all the answers with him to the grave, no doubt."

"Some," Stephanie admitted, "but not all. However, there are some new questions that have come up. Like, where had he been hiding all this time? Who might his accomplices have been? There's still plenty to dig into."

"Wait a minute; you said it blew up? That buyboat was electric-powered; how could it blow up?"

Stephanie nodded, "It was. But it also had a huge lithium-ion battery bank. Under the right circumstances, even the small ones can catch fire and explode. There have been hundreds of fires linked to lithium-ion-powered bicycles in this year alone."

"I'll be damned; Baloney was right. He said they could blow, but I thought it was just another 'Baloneyism.' You know how he gets sometimes."

"A 'Baloneyism.' That's a new one, but I need to remember it," Stephanie said, shaking her head.

"Maybe a new phrase, but nothing really new behind it. And let's go back to the explosion. I read an article about those bike battery fires; almost all of them happened while they were being charged. Unless Han had a cord a mile long, it sounds like this one wasn't plugged in."

"No," she admitted. "We think he was making a run for it and was pushing the boat to its limits."

"Why do you think he was leaving?"

"Because that's what the tipster said."

"What tipster?" Sandy asked, confused.

"The one that called the Coast Guard in Cape Charles who said he spotted the *Sandra T* running south down by Kiptopeke State Park. The Coasties were searching for him and were only a couple of miles behind when they saw an explosion. Wait... You're right. I was only focusing on the fact that it was the *Sandra T*. After they saw the explosion, they reached the scene and picked up a life ring with the boat's name painted on it. One of them recalled seeing it was connected to a BOLO. That's how I got called, but how did *they* get called? And why did they get called directly instead of 911 or the sheriff? How could the tipster have known Han was fleeing?"

Sandy leaned back and took a sip of coffee, and began thinking out loud. "If you were the tipster, you'd call the Coast Guard because they have boats. That part could be innocent enough. Who else other than law enforcement did you send those BOLOs out to? Your caller knew you were looking for that boat. There are two ways they could have known that; either because they'd seen the BOLO or maybe because they knew Han and what he was up to. But assuming your tipster was out on the water near Han, how could they have recognized the *Sandra T* in the dark? You'd have had to have been right on their stern with a spotlight to read the name.

"No, like I said, he took a lot of answers with him, and as you said, he raised more questions by dying. Someone ratted him out, and I'd bet it was someone close that needed him out of the way or didn't want him talking. By calling it in, this would have meant they wanted him caught or found. Instead, somebody blew up that boat."

She nodded. "Sounds plausible."

Sandy frowned. "More than plausible; it's damned likely. By calling it in, they made sure that the Coast Guard would be close by when it blew. They needed Han to be found and identified. They wanted the digging to stop."

It was Stephanie's turn to frown. "Only, they didn't know me. There's a lot more to this, but I can't tell you. It goes way beyond Han."

Sandy tilted his head slightly. "All the way to Wallops?"

She nodded. "And beyond. Way beyond."

"Hey! Aren't you looking better," Stephanie said. She and Sandy had walked over to *Lady Dawn* to check on Baloney after they finished breakfast. They found him sitting on the top deck with Rikki, again staring out toward the Inside Passage.

He turned and looked at her. "Feelin' better, too. What brings ya over this way, Steph?"

"Chasing bad guys. Or, in this case, picking up pieces of bad guys. Han got flushed out of wherever he was hiding last night and was fleeing in the *Sandra T* when it exploded last night. Took out him and his two guys."

"Ya see, Hack, I told ya that nothin' good will come from changin' a buyboat over ta electric..." Suddenly Baloney's face went blank like he was starting off into the distance. "It was Han. His boat."

Stephanie nodded. "Yes, we made a positive ID..."

"No, Steph, I'm talkin' about at the barge. I kept seein' it in like a cloud, just outta focus. Couldn't remember exactly what I saw.

"When I turned *Oar House* around and came back, the lights caught the stern of a boat pullin' away from the far side. I only saw it for a split second, and now when ya said it blew up, that kinda jogged my memory. It was that *Sandra T*. They were there that night. At least the boat was there."

"You said there were two guys on the barge with Asian accents."

"More'n Asian accents, they were Asian. I got a look at 'em as we pulled alongside. Cohen was burnin' every light in th' salon, an' the blinds were all open, lightin' them up pretty good. I can still remember their faces."

Stephanie took out her phone and scrolled through some photos. She held the screen up to Baloney, asking, "Is this one of those two guys that were on the barge that night?"

"Yeah! How'd ya get that? Wow, he doesn't look too good."

Rikki said, "That's because he's dead. He's the one that Tyrell shot, the one who was trying to stab you."

"He's Korean?" Baloney asked.

Stephanie shook her head. "No, he's Chinese, or at least he *was* Chinese. A Triad gang member."

Baloney went back to staring off at the water again. Only this time, he was saying softly, "Then if I had kept goin' and not come back ta check on that barge, Betty'd still be alive. Han musta recognized the boat. That's how he knew ta send somebody for us."

Sandy said equally as softly as Baloney, "If you hadn't gone back, Betty would have been disappointed in you. It was what all of us would have done because it was the responsible thing to do. You had no way of knowing if anyone had been hurt; you didn't have a choice; you had to go back."

Baloney turned to him and said, "I got Betty killed, Sandy."

Sandy saw it then, in his eyes and on his face, the grief that Baloney had been denying all along. "No, Bill, you didn't. That asswipe Cohen did when he let that drunk girl steer into the side of that barge. There's more to this than we're allowed to know."

"Whatta ya mean?"

Sandy replied, "We're getting left out of the loop on some things."

"What?"

"If I knew, Bill, I'd tell you." He looked over at Stephanie, who was sharing a guilty look with Rikki.

Stephanie said, "Bill, I wish I could tell you more, but I can't. It's a matter of national security. What I can tell you is that it wasn't just about hitting a barge."

The realization dawned on his face as he recalled something he saw. "Nah, it was about those things on the deck, wasn't it? That scissor lift-lookin' thingy and that leather stingray. Those were the only weird things I saw on that barge that looked outta place."

"Wait, you saw a leather stingray?" Stephanie asked.

"Yeah. Just for a second as the lights swept over th' barge deck. That's about the best way ta describe it. Big, like ten or twelve feet across. Had a lot ah gills on its back. Sitting over on the deck next ta that lift thing. They were both in front ah that container, like they just got unloaded from it."

"Can you draw what you saw?"

"I'm no Picasso, but I can give it a try, sure."

Sandy wasn't satisfied with what little information they were getting. "Steph, Rik and Casey found that barge, right? So, why don't you search it?"

Stephanie stared blankly at him.

"Don't blame either of those two; they wouldn't say anything. But you just did by your silence. You can't search it, can you? Because you don't have it." Suddenly the answer came to him. "Those two found it and went running up to see you. It couldn't have taken them that long.

"Then, in the short amount of time between when they found it and when you could all fly back there together, something happened to it. Couldn't have been that it sped away; barges don't go fast. There has to be something that keeps you from being able to search it for some reason. I'm guessing that it's on the bottom of the ocean. But it wouldn't be in deep enough water to prevent you from being able to dive on it, so something else must've happened.

"Let's see, a rocket got blown up, and now the boat that Gilligan saw at that barge also got blown up. Three guesses as to what happened to that barge, and your first two don't count."

"Wait, what rocket?" Baloney asked.

Sandy said, "A big one up at Wallops. Super-secret payload. It got brought down by something they hadn't seen before, something that scares the hell out of them. Super stealthy and super lethal. And unless I miss my guess, you're the only living person on our side that has ever seen it. That's why they want a drawing of it."

Sandy stopped to think for a minute before continuing, "So, a rocket large enough to carry several satellites gets taken out by some Koreans and some Chinese gang members. Any guesses as to which side of Korea Han was from or where that cargo—let's just go ahead and figure it was satellites—was headed?"

Stephanie held out her hand with her palm up in a stop motion. "Sandy, before you say anything more, I have to tell you all that I need to detain you all right now until someone from the National Security Agency can come and have a talk with you. Please shut off all of your cell phones until that can happen." She stared at Sandy. "How did you figure out so much?"

"You can write fiction, or you can write good fiction. Good fiction requires doing a lot of research and a little reasoning. Some of what you learn along the way is bound to stick in your brain..."

WHILE THEY WAITED, they all moved inside since Jack Miller had cranked up the pile driver again. Then it took the trio from the NSA an hour and a half to arrive, two field agents and a sketch artist. First, they questioned Baloney on what he had seen and the others on what they had heard. Then they were all sworn to secrecy in a well-rehearsed preamble that included words like prison, treason, and other assorted phrases intended to evoke fear and guarantee compliance.

Sandy was less than impressed. "You can say all the scary things you can think of to intimidate the masses, but when it gets right down to it, what inspires people to keep silent is their love for this country. Period. If they don't have that, there's not much you can say that will have as much of an effect.

"Bill lost his wife and almost his own life. We all lost a dear friend. It's the hope that she didn't die in vain and that Bill hasn't suffered for nothing that will keep us from talking outside this group."

"Not even within this group," the NSA guy warned.

Sandy frowned. "Right. You wouldn't want us to share what we already all know with each other again. Might make for more paperwork headaches for you, especially if we figure something out that you haven't."

"You need to remember what I said about felonies and prison, Morgan. And keep your mouth shut."

"And you need to remember what I said about our friend dying for nothing and do something about it. We're missing one guy from that barge, and that stingray didn't get built by itself. Plus, I doubt that Han blew himself up. There are more missing pieces to this, and so far, it seems like you're chasing your tails and not stopping the bad guys that are still out there running around. From where I stand, it looks like you can use all the help you can get."

15

SUNSET GOODBYES

S heriff Bromwell received an early morning phone call from Fong, wanting an update.

"The feds are all kinds of pissed off over Han. Kinda hard to question a corpse." Bromwell figured that Fong had arranged Han's "accident" since he was no longer a client and had moved over into the liability column. Loose ends get trimmed.

"Are they looking beyond Han?"

"I don't know. We ain't exactly on buddy-buddy terms; you know what I mean?"

"I know that I pay you to find out such things. If you cannot, then your value to me decreases, perhaps as much as Han's did. That is not something that you would want to happen. You need to keep that in mind."

~

"I been thinkin', Sandy, about spreadin' Betty's ashes. I know some people like keepin' them around a while, but that ain't for me. I know where an' when I wanna do it."

The two men were back out on the top deck of *Lady Dawn* a few minutes after five, an hour after Jack Miller's crew had knocked off for the day. Each had a bottle of their favorite beer in hand, but neither had made much of a dent in theirs.

"Whatever you think, Bill. Wherever, whenever."

"When we were on that damn booze cruise, she said she wanted ta see more sunsets from our boat, her an' me. It's a spot just offshore, about a half hour from here, at slow speed, an' that's how I wanna go. In the *Dolphin*, with Bobby runnin' the boat. We go up a little early, an' at sunset, I'll spread her ashes on the water. It's what I know she'd want ta happen. Ya mind goin' with me?"

"Of course, I'll go. I think there are a lot of other folks and boats that'll want to go as well. Why don't you call Bobby and get him set up? He'll probably want to get the word out."

"Good idea. A lot ah people liked Betty."

"Yes, they did."

OVERNIGHT, the word spread about Betty's last cruise, and more boats and crews signed on. By the time the procession left *Mallard Cove* with the *Golden Dolphin* in the lead, it had become almost a hundred boats long. All of the *Cove*'s charter fleet, the *Tuna Hunters*' boats, along with many of the others that also fish in the lower bay, attended. Many of the production and office staff of *Tuna Hunter Productions* hitched rides on whatever boats had room, including Eric Cottell's Scarab that he and Tommy ran. Rev, Debbie, and her parents rode on the *Golden Dolphin* along with B2, Sandy, and Baloney. The remainder of *Casey's Crew* and the crew from *Lady Dawn*, Angel, and Mimi all rode together on *Sharke*, a seventy-five-foot Jarrett Bay sport fisherman owned by the Shaw's and Eric Clarke, another member of *Casey's Crew*.

With Baloney's permission, a *Tuna Hunters* drone filmed the procession leaving the *Cove* area and arriving at Betty's final resting spot. It hovered overhead as Rev said a short sermon, then Baloney spread Betty's ashes as the sun set over that part of the Eastern Shore, just as it had that night a few weeks before. One by one, the rest of the boats passed by the stern of the *Dolphin*, their crews throwing individual flowers into the water in the growing dusk.

Back at *Mallard Cove*, the *Beach Bar* had closed to the public as they had prepared a reception for those that had made the trip up to honor Betty. *Sharke* was one of the first boats back in, as Murph and Lindsay wanted to check over the details before Baloney and his family arrived. Then they went over to help Baloney get off the *Dolphin* since he was still far from fully recovered, and the day had taken a lot out of him. As they watched B2 back the old sportfish into her slip, they saw a sheriff's car roll past in the parking lot, its blue strobe lights flashing, followed soon by another unmarked car.

"What the hell, now," Murph groaned. It didn't take long to get an answer, as Barry, the dockmaster, came to tell them that while everyone was gone, Eric Cottell's Hatteras, *Providence,* had been stolen. With no one left on the dock, there had been no witnesses to the theft. It had simply vanished without a trace. They didn't even know in which direction it had gone.

"IF I HADN'T HEARD that Han was dead, I'd suspect him. It was likely one of his accomplices, looking to steal the upgrades I made on my fuel emulsion system!" Eric was furious, and rightfully so, as his home while in the US as well as his technology had all disappeared, along with his and Tommy's passports, which they'd need to get back into the Bahamas.

"You need to be very careful about throwing around accusations like that; it could get you in trouble," Sheriff Bromwell said.

"I could be in trouble? Me? Are you serious? This place was supposed to be fun and safe. So far, since I arrived, there have been three murders, one attempted murder, one boat explosion with three more deaths, another boat stolen and burned, and now my own yacht stolen!"

"Yeah, and as you pointed out so well, it all happened after you got here. Come to think of it, you knew all of the victims and had talked to them shortly before those things happened. You're moving up fast on the persons of interest list," Bromwell said.

Eric exploded. "I did not know all of the victims, I'd barely met half of them! And I was out in the funeral procession with a hundred other boats when *Providence* was stolen, and they're all witnesses to that!"

"But you got real cozy with Han real fast since he was gonna be your customer. And settin' up such a good alibi is good thinkin' for pullin' off an insurance scam. I think I'll just take you and your mate's passports until we get this all settled." Bromwell had on his best smug look.

"Well, now, that's going to be hard to do, isn't it, since they are both aboard *Providence*! If you want them, then go find my boat!"

Murph, Rikki, and Stephanie had been standing behind the sheriff, listening to the conversation. Before Bromwell could reply, Stephanie stepped up.

"Nice to see you take such a personal interest in this particular boat theft, Sheriff. By the way, Mr. Cottell is a material witness in an ongoing FBI investigation, so unless you have evidence of this alleged insurance scam, we will take over responsibility for him."

"What investigation, Baker?" Bromwell suddenly looked nervous.

"Well, Sheriff, it's an ongoing investigation, so I'm not at liberty to discuss that with you." She'd put an emphasis on the word "you" to see if he would squirm. He did.

"What is it with you, Baker? You keep sticking your nose into a lot of things that are in my jurisdiction, and I'm not gonna stand for it."

"Well, Sheriff, when you start protecting your witnesses better and fully investigating all your local boat thefts, then maybe I won't have to."

"But you don't have any jurisdiction in any of this unless it involves two or more states. An' this don't."

"That would be true if this was a separate incident and not part of an investigation into a larger, far-reaching conspiracy, which is all I can say to you at this time." She crossed her arms as she stared at him.

The sheriff looked around at the faces that were all staring at him, then said, "C'mon, Aldrich, let's get out of here. If the FBI wants to take over this mess, let's let them have it." The two walked away, but not before Aldrich gave Stephanie a questioning look as he passed by.

"Now what?" Eric asked Stephanie. "How do you plan on getting my boat back and catching whoever did this?"

Rikki answered instead. "I have an idea. What is the top speed and range of your boat, Eric?"

"A little under twenty knots, but right now, the range is probably less than twenty miles. We had run the tanks down on purpose, wanting to change the fuel filters and start them with brand-new fuel. We had planned on doing that today and fueling this afternoon, but then this funeral thing came up, and we put all that off until tomorrow. So, they aren't going to get far, whoever they are, unless they have a mobile fuel station in their back pocket. Most fuel places around here are closed until the morning."

Stephanie said, "That's hardly enough range to get across the mouth of the bay over to Virginia Beach, and if they are after your fuel things as you suspect, they're going to want to get them off your boat quickly. I'm assuming they can't do that with the boat still running."

He shook his head. "Not only that, but if they've run more than a few minutes, the engine rooms will be unbearably hot, and they'll need to wait until they cool down a bit first."

Rikki said, "We can take the seaplane up at dawn. We'll start by checking the docks on the ocean side first, then cross over and do the bay side. Not a lot of places where it could be within twenty miles. It's not like this is southeast Florida, all bumper-to-bumper docks. And that hull shape is pretty distinctive." Rikki knew Hatteras boats well, as she and Cindy owned and lived aboard another model, but they'd researched most of the others before making their choice.

Stephanie said, "Meanwhile, I'll alert the Coast Guard about *Providence* being stolen. Maybe they'll get lucky again."

Murph had been silent up until now, mostly thinking of any way he could keep this from becoming another public relations nightmare for *Mallard Cove*. So far, he wasn't having any success. "Eric, these two will get your boat back. They're the best at what they do." Secretly he was thinking to himself that they'll find it, if it isn't at the bottom of the bay or the Atlantic. "Meanwhile, you and Tommy are welcome to stay aboard my houseboat; we have a couple of guest staterooms."

"I probably won't get much sleep tonight, but thank you, we'll take you up on that. I'll take the Scarab out at dawn and see if I can spot *Providence* myself. If you can make a list of all the fuel docks within twenty miles, I'll start with those first."

"I'll do better than that; I'll go with you," Murph said. "Local knowledge can save a lot of propellers from all the oyster bars around here. In the meantime, let's get back over to the reception and show our support for Baloney. He's going to need it."

FONG WAS ABOUT to slow *Providence* before making the turn into his narrow channel that the previous owner had cut through the marshy edge of land at the edge of the bay. But before he could pull the throttle back, one of the engines began "galloping," surging before finally quitting altogether.

Fong swore, then throttled back the one operating engine. He told the man he brought with him to steer straight, then went down into the cockpit. With a penlight, he looked through the little windows in the deck at the manual fuel gauges on top of the tanks. Each read empty. He swore again, then climbed back up to the flybridge.

"Problems?" the man asked.

"Yes," Fong replied tersely, pushing the man away from the steering wheel. The boat had already started drifting to starboard, into the side with the dead engine as the good engine pushed it off center.

Fortunately for Fong, he still had enough open water between the boat and the channel that he was able to throttle up the operating engine. While it first began pushing the hull to starboard again, eventually, it built up enough speed to allow the rudders to counteract the offset thrust and the drag of the dead engine's prop, steering sluggishly back to a centerline.

So long as he could maintain this speed, Fong knew he should be able to navigate the narrow, shallow cut. But he also knew that once he was inside his tiny basin, stopping and maneuvering on one engine was going to get very dicey, as the boat would only want to pivot, not run straight. Though it wasn't like he had a choice, as he had already turned into the mouth of the cut, and he was now committed.

Halfway down the channel, the dreaded diesel "gallop" now began with the remaining engine.

"No, no, no, NOOOOO!!" Fong yelled right before that engine died. To be able to stop in the basin, he had held the speed down to barely above what made it maneuverable on one engine. He held his breath as the boat now slowed as it coasted. Then his worst nightmare became a reality as the hull began to drift to starboard as the rudders became ineffective again.

For a few seconds, Fong thought he'd have enough room to clear the cut and coast into the basin. But then the drift became more pronounced, and the bow hit and dug into the mud at the side of the channel. The inertia of the 55,000-pound vessel shoved it several feet beyond its contact with the shore. As the bow dug in and stopped its forward momentum, the remaining kinetic energy pushed the stern sideways. The hull pivoted at the bow until the rudders and props came into contact with the opposite side of the narrow cut and buried themselves in its mud. The basin was now essentially blocked from all traffic.

"Damn, damn, DAMN!" Fong swore. He had wanted to remove the devices and then take the boat out into the bay to scuttle it under cover of darkness. That wasn't going to be possible now, as they were at peak flood tide. With the water receding, it would be almost twelve hours until it would be this high again. Even if he were able to dislodge and re-float *Providence* by then, it would be broad daylight at that point.

He was certain that by dawn, every marine unit on the Chesapeake would be looking for the boat. Hopefully, it was far enough into the brush not to be spotted unless someone was looking straight down the cut. And from far out in the bay, they would only get a slight glimpse of the hull, probably not enough to identify it. He hoped.

16

CUSTOMER SERVICE

The next day, at 5:30 a.m., Accomack County Airport, ESVA

"THE LAST TIME you two did this, you almost got yourselves blown up. Can we try not to have that happen again this time?" Stephanie asked as she climbed across the Cessna's float and up into the cabin. Casey and Rikki were already aboard, fastening their seatbelts.

Rikki said, "C'mon, Steph, where's your sense of adventure?" She turned and grinned at her from the copilot seat.

"I left it at home. I brought along my sense of caution instead."

"Okay, here's the plan," Casey said. "We'll head south on the ocean side, and work our way down to the tip of ESVA, then back up the bay side. I doubt it will be in any of the marinas; probably more likely to be at a private dock and hopefully not way out in the ocean meeting another boat." He didn't need to add *or scuttled* since the others were already thinking it.

They stuck to the plan, passing over the spot where Baloney had scattered Betty's ashes the night before about ten minutes into the flight. They only had one false alarm a little before that, a similar

Hatteras up Parting Creek, off the Machipongo River, but it turned out to be a fifty-eight-footer.

Making the turn over *Mallard Cove*, Casey climbed to 2,000 feet as he transitioned north. It was slightly hazy, and the additional five hundred feet allowed them to see both sides of the bay. As they passed over Kiptopeke State Park with its famous breakwater made from sunken concrete ships, Rikki leaned forward in her seat, refocusing her binoculars.

"Turn offshore, Case; I've got her. We don't want to fly directly overhead, or they might spook. You two are not going to believe where she's sitting."

"Where?" Stephanie asked.

"The old Outerbridge place. Looks like she's stuck in the cut, about a hundred yards from where Baloney's Merritt burned."

Stephanie thought back to that night when she and her group stormed the property after receiving a text from Casey. She knew there were things that happened that were kept from her before he sent that text. It was likely Casey and his friends had been on the scene and then left prior to sending her that tip. She suspected they might have even been the ones who set fire to what was now Baloney's Merritt but, at the time, belonged to a counterfeiter and drug manufacturer with a deadly Chinese customer... a customer... Bromwell mentioned last night that Han was a customer of Cottell's. How could he...

"Rik, call Murph for me. He's supposed to be out with Cottell this morning."

"Uh, okay?"

"When you get him, have him put Eric on the phone."

A minute later, a curious-looking Rikki passed the phone back to Stephanie. "Hi, Mr. Cottell? Stephanie Baker with the FBI... Okay, Eric. I need to know, did you mention to Sheriff Bromwell or anyone close to him that Han was your customer... You're certain... Okay, please keep this confidential like that other conversation we had... Yes, I'm hoping to give you some good news later today. Thanks, and goodbye."

As Stephanie handed the phone back, Rikki demanded, "What was up with that?"

"Another piece of the puzzle falling into place. Case, can you land at the *Cove Club*? I'm going to get my team to meet me there."

～

BALONEY WAS ONCE AGAIN in his favorite new perch, that aft-facing chair on *Lady Dawn*'s top deck. He was in a dour mood since he hadn't been allowed to join in on the hunt for *Providence*. He was making his displeasure very clear to Sandy.

"Yeah, well, then you know how I must feel, Gilligan, since I was assigned to keep you company here."

"Keep me company, my butt! More yer actin' like th' warden in a prison lockdown."

"Well, somebody has to ride herd on you. Look how yesterday's little jaunt took it all out of you. We don't need a repeat of that. The sooner you heal and get back to one hundred percent, the faster I can get back to my own life."

"Who says ya can't now?"

"Everybody! You need somebody to stick with you, and it wasn't fair to make Andrea do it all the time."

Baloney glared at him. "Why's it gotta be you, ya hack?"

Sandy returned the glare. "Because I drew the short straw!"

The two men continued their glaring contest until the slightest hint of a smile appeared in the corner of Baloney's mouth. He quickly replaced it with a cigar. This one stayed stationary, letting Sandy know that his friend wasn't truly angry. At least, not very much.

Baloney took the cigar out of his mouth and stared at it. "Ya know, hack, I'm startin' ta realize how much my life has changed. I never lit one ah these while I was at th' dock 'cause that was one ah Betty's strictest rules. I guess it don't matter now." His shoulders sagged as he rolled the tobacco cylinder in his fingers.

"The hell it doesn't! You light that, and I swear, I'll deck you myself. Don't you dare dishonor her memory by breaking that rule, you hear me? You'd never forgive yourself. And I wouldn't either."

Baloney looked up at Sandy as his eyes began to well up. He didn't say anything; he didn't need to. Sandy remembered how the sadness had come over him in waves after his wife passed. Sometimes it would hit so suddenly, so unexpectedly, just as it was hitting Baloney now.

Baloney put the cigar back in his shirt pocket and wiped his eyes with his hands. "Yer right. Thanks."

"Two things to remember about life, Baloney: the first is, I'm always right. And second, if I go to use the 'head' after lunch and there's no beer left in my glass, you just got stuck with the tab!"

Sandy grinned, and Baloney started to laugh.

"Don't make me laugh, Hack; it still hurts ta laugh!"

Their conversation was interrupted by the sound of an approaching plane. Looking right, they saw the seaplane touch down by the mouth of the inside passage. Casey kept it up on step until he was opposite *Lady Dawn*, then he let the floats settle into the water, taxiing toward the ramp at the *Cove Club*. Extending the landing gear, he drove the turboprop up the concrete ramp, stopping short of the helipad.

From their perch on the upper deck, they could see Stephanie hop out, then race over and disappear through the trees at the gate. After the seaplane's engine finally came to a stop, Casey and Rikki hopped out. They put wedge-shaped rubber chocks on both sides of the main landing gear's wheels before walking over to *Lady Dawn* and joining Sandy and Bill.

"You two are back already?" Sandy asked.

Casey nodded. "We found *Providence*, and Stephanie put together a team to go and get her back."

"Was she still in one piece?" Baloney asked. "And where was she?"

"As far as we could see, she is," Rikki replied. "She's a hundred yards away from where your Merritt burned."

"What? Where that Outerbridge fella had her? I heard they auctioned off that property."

"Maybe it just passed from one bad hand into another," Rikki suggested.

"At least I can give Cottell some good news. Here he an' Murph come!" Baloney pointed over to where Casey had just landed. Eric's Scarab was now entering the passage.

Rikki caught the part about Baloney sharing the news with Eric as if he had been the one to find the Hatteras. She smiled slightly, not minding that her friend was apparently intending to take the credit. It was a sign that he was getting back to his old self, at least partially.

ERIC AND MURPH tied up alongside *Lady Dawn* and climbed the stairs to the upper deck. Murph said, "We saw you landing, Case. I told Eric that if you were back this early, you must have some news."

Baloney said, "Yeah, great news, we found her! Tell 'em, Rik."

Rik glanced sideways at Casey, who was grinning at what Baloney said. "Yes, we did find *Providence*, Eric, and she appears to be intact. Looks like she's grounded in the mud in the cut leading to the old Outerbridge property. Stephanie and her FBI team are en route to seize it and arrest the thieves."

"That's very good news." Only this didn't come from Cottell; instead, Detective Aldrich had said it. He was at the top of the staircase, having arrived to check in with Baloney to see if any more of his memory had returned. "I'll let the sheriff know so that he can send some deputies to assist." He looked down and began texting.

"I wouldn't do that. If Special Agent Baker wanted help from the SO, I'm sure she'd have asked for it already," Rikki said.

Aldrich looked up and said, "We still don't need any cheating spouses investigated, Jenkins, so you can keep your suggestions to yourself." Then he turned and left, forgetting about Baloney for the moment.

∿

THE SHERIFF STARED at the screen on his phone, then reached into his pocket for the burner. While making a quick call, he sped off in the direction of the old Outerbridge place.

FONG STARED at the phone and hit the end button. He glanced around quickly, taking stock of his situation. The two men inside the building were expendable, especially the one who had been spotted on the barge and later failed to kill Bigmouth on his boat. Still looking around, he wished that he could have taken the black Escalade, but he wasn't certain that there was time, and he also wasn't sure if the FBI had its description.

Looking out toward the Hatteras and felt a twinge of regret at having to leave his mechanic. But the inflatable was tied alongside the yacht, so there was no other way to reach him in time. Besides, the man was not yet a full Triad member, so Fong was not loyally bound to him. As for the other two, sometimes you have to sacrifice some pawns to save a king.

Fong now slipped over into the woods beside the warehouse, going to the old, dilapidated shed where he had hidden the electric motocross bike. He mounted the bike and took off down a trail that led to a neighboring property that he also owned. In the driveway was an older Kia with dark-tinted windows. He drove down the bush-lined driveway, out onto US 13, where he turned south. He'd be in his Virginia Beach safe house in less than an hour.

Two minutes later, he passed Bromwell, who was going in the opposite direction. He thought about calling him and telling him not to go to the property but then thought better of it. Bromwell's safety hinged on Fong's men staying silent as well. Two minutes later, he passed another sheriff's car, an unmarked one. It was also speeding in the opposite direction. So far, so good, he thought. If only his luck would hold past the CBBT.

STEPHANIE and her team of five agents cautiously made their way down the driveway. Fortunately, four of them had been on the Outerbridge raid, so they were familiar with the territory. They split up before they reached the warehouse, two going left to check Fong's house while she and her other three agents cut through the brush to the rear corner of the warehouse.

Advancing as a single unit, they reached the front corner of the building thirty seconds later. Fong's two men were smoking by the huge, open garage door. Their surprise at seeing the FBI only lasted for a split second as one quickly began firing at the agents. He was cut down almost as fast, but the other man was now running for the same woods where Fong had gone.

"Williams, take your men and clear the warehouse; I'll go after this one," Stephanie yelled, running across the gravel parking area. She was only seconds behind the man as he entered the woods.

Stephanie was moving forward more cautiously now, as the man now had a lot of cover to hide behind to be able to ambush her. A hundred feet into the woods, she spotted the man sprawled on the ground, struggling to get up. He'd tripped over a tree root, and his pistol had come out of his hand. It lay on the ground, five feet away from him.

"Freeze! You make one move toward that gun, and I'll shoot! Stay down."

The man complied, though she could see him weighing his odds of safely reaching the gun. As she stood behind him, catching her breath, a shot rang out from close behind her, the bullet hitting her suspect in the head, killing him instantly.

Sheriff Bromwell walked past a stunned Stephanie, picking up the gun off the ground.

"What the hell did you do that for," Stephanie demanded. "I had him down at gunpoint!"

"Well, my story is he was reaching for this gun. Baker, you've been such a pain in my ass, and that ends right now. And unfortunately, you weren't fast enough on your trigger, so he shot and killed you." Now Bromwell squatted down, mimicking the angle from where the suspect would have shot. Aiming for Stephanie's head, above her body armor. As he began to squeeze the trigger, someone behind Stephanie yelled, "Drop it, Sheriff!"

The distraction gave Stephanie the split second that she needed to move out of the path of the bullet, which flew past her left ear. Another shot rang out, this bullet hitting Bromwell in the throat, above his own vest. He dropped the gun and grabbed his neck where his jugular vein had been hit. Blood was spurting out of the wound as Bromwell fell over backward.

"You okay, Baker?" Aldrich asked, keeping his pistol aimed at Bromwell, who was quickly bleeding out.

"Yeah, thanks. Did you hear all of that?"

"Even better, I got it all on my body-cam."

EPILOGUE

A few hours after the raid, Stephanie stopped by *Lady Dawn* on her way over to her office and a few pounds of paperwork that was going to take days to write. But she had discovered information that she wanted to share with Baloney. She found him in the salon with Sandy, Casey, Dawn, Murph, and one very anxious Eric, who wanted to go over to *Providence* and bring her back to *Mallard Cove*.

Unfortunately, she explained that it was still a crime scene, and wouldn't be released until almost dark. But they had managed to free the yacht at high tide, using the inflatable's engine to push her stern back into deep water, then pull her bow off the bank. Ironically, she was now sitting in the same slip where Baloney's Merritt had burned.

"You're going to need a fuel truck and a few wrenches, too. Fong's mechanic had both emulsion units unhooked and ready to be offloaded."

Eric sighed. "At least they're still there. And it's not like I haven't installed them before. I'm just glad she's still afloat."

Stephanie continued, "Fong's mechanical guy was just that and not one of his soldiers. Hearing all the gunfire, he had come up on deck to find a couple of rifles pointed at him from shore and a Coast Guard RHIB with several heavily armed crewmen tying up on the bay side. Boy, was he pissed at not having been given a heads-up so he could've run.

"It's a good thing we had him on camera because he was spilling his guts faster than any of us could have written it down. He's looking for a deal. He said that this guy"—she held up a picture of the man Bromwell had shot for Baloney to see—"is the second man who attacked all four here on the boats."

Baloney sighed. "Yeah, he was th' other guy onna barge. So he killed Betty. Glad the sonofabitch is dead, just wished I'd ah done it."

Sandy asked, "What about Fong?"

Stephanie replied, "Vanished. I'd like to say we've probably seen the last of him, but you never know."

Sandy said, "I saw on the internet that there was a leak that said there were four spy satellites on that rocket, and all four were lost. It said that they were supposed to have been stationed over North Korea."

Stephanie smiled as she shrugged.

Sandy continued, "Then I saw a picture of a launch from Cape Canaveral a couple of days after that of the exact same rocket model. The picture got taken down pretty fast, and there's no more mention of it anywhere. Why am I getting the feeling that the Feds might have suspected an attempt would be made on the Wallops rocket, and they used it as bait to draw fire?"

Stephanie frowned, "I like you better when you're writing fiction, Sandy."

"Wasn't that what I was doing?" he asked, very innocent sounding.

"Just don't put that in a book, okay? I'm not saying that's what happened, but you wouldn't want to get anybody poking around, thinking it might be, right?"

He chuckled. "Already sworn to secrecy, remember? Treason, prison, execution, yada, yada, yada..."

"And if Aldrich hadn't overheard you guys talking, Bromwell wouldn't have known and tipped off Fong. But I guess I owe him for saving my life and for not having to open one very long investigation into the sheriff. Though we're still going to look into several of his deputies."

Sandy said, "I'm just glad he's gone. The last loose thread that needed to be dealt with."

"Not quite, ya hack. Ya still owe me that case ah Kalik. Me an' Bobby'll be bringin' *Dorado* home next week, an' th' fridge is empty."

"It will be waiting on you when you tie up."

"Sounds good. An' speakin' of beer, ya wanna go ta England? I've got first-class tickets, and the beer is free up front in th' plane..."

AUTHOR NOTES: Eric Cottell is a real person and a pal of mine who lives in Nassau, Bahamas. Nonox Ltd. is also real, as is his emulsion system, exactly as I've described it. And *Providence*? Also real and a beauty!

GLOSSARY

I grew up on the water in South Florida, and I have an extensive boating background. I've worked on boats, built them, re-built them, and spent a good amount of time in boatyards. I've always loved boats, and ever since I was a pre-teenager, I haven't gone longer than six months without owning at least one. Most of my friends are boaters, too. So it's easy for me to forget that not everyone is as familiar with the jargon as my friends and me, which is something that I've now been reminded of on more than one occasion. (My apologies to those readers that I ended up sending to the dictionary!) To make amends, here's a (growing) list of uniquely nautical terms and words that have been included in several of my books. Bear in mind that these definitions are based on my own usage and experience. Things can be different from one region to another. For instance, you can fish for stripers in Montauk, New York, but here in Virginia, we fish for rockfish. But the true name for the target species is "striped bass."

So, here are the definitions of some of the more confusing words, at least as I know them. We'll start with a half dozen simple ones, then move on to those that are more complex:

- **Bow:** the front of the boat.
- **Stern:** back of the boat.
- **Port:** the left side of the boat.
- **Starboard:** the right side of the boat.
- **Aft:** the rear of the boat.
- **Forward:** (fore) the front of the boat.
- **Bow Thruster:** a propeller in a tube that is mounted from side to side through the bow below the waterline, allowing the captain more maneuverability and control when docking especially in adverse winds and current. Powered by an electric or hydraulic motor.
- **Bulkhead:** boat wall.
- **Center Console:** a type of boat with a raised helm console in the middle of the boat with space on each side to walk around. Most also incorporate a built-in bench seat or cooler seat in the front.
- **Chine:** the longitudinal area running fore and aft where the bottom meets the side. It can be rounded or "sharp." They hurt when the boat rocks and it meets your head when you are swimming next to it. Trust me on that.
- **Circle Hook:** a fishhook designed to get caught in the corner of a fish's mouth. Greatly reduces the mortality of fish that are released or that break the line.
- **Citation:** at an airport, it's a type of jet made by Cessna. But here in Virginia, it's a slip of paper suitable for framing, issued by the state confirming that you caught a fish that's considered large for its particular species. Or it can be a speeding ticket, either on water or land. I like the fish kind better.
- **Covering Board:** a flat surface at the top of a gunwale usually made out of teak or fiberglass, that's used as a step for boarding and for mounting recessed rod holders.
- **Deck:** what floors on boats are called.

- **Fighting Chair:** a specialized chair that can be turned to face a fish. Mounted on a sturdy stanchion with a built-in gimbal, the chair allows the angler to use the attached footrest to use their legs and body to gain more leverage on a large fish. Most of today's fighting chairs are based on the design by my late friend John Rybovich.
- **Fish Box:** a built-in storage box for the day's catch. They can be either elevated in the stern, or in the deck with a flush-mounted lid. Some of the higher-end sportfish boats have cooling systems or automatic ice makers that continually add ice throughout the trip.
- **Fishing Cockpit:** the lower aft deck on a sport fisherman that usually contains a fighting chair, fish box, baitwell, and tackle center. Surrounded on three sides by the gunwales and the stern. The cockpit deck is usually just above the waterline, with scuppers that drain overboard. Can get flooded when backing down hard on a big fish.
- **Flying Bridge (Flybridge):** a permanently mounted helm area on top of the wheelhouse. Can be open or enclosed.
- **Following Sea:** when the waves are moving toward the boat from behind the stern.
- **Gaff:** a large, usually barbless hook at the end of a pole, used for landing fish. They come in different sizes and lengths.
- **Gangway (Gangplank):** a removable ramp or set of stairs attached to the side of larger boats to allow easier access for boarding from a dock. Usually hinged to allow for tide variation.
- **Gear:** marine transmission which has forward, neutral, and reverse.
- **Gimbal:** there are a few types, but the ones in my books are rod holders with swivels built into fighting chairs.
- **Gin Pole:** a vertical pole next to the gunwale usually rigged with a block and tackle and used for hauling large

fish aboard. These used to be quite common until John Rybovich invented the transom door fifty years ago.

- **Gunwale (pronounced gun-nul):** aft side area of a boat above the waterline, also the area on either side of a fishing cockpit.
- **Hatch:** a hole in a deck or bulkhead with a cover that may be hinged or completely removable. On a sport fisherman, the door into the wheelhouse may be called either a hatch or a door.
- **Head:** a bathroom, or a marine toilet.
- **Helm:** the area that includes the steering and engine controls. In many sportfishing boats, the controls are mounted on a helm pod, a wood box with radiused edges that juts out of a cabinet or bulkhead.
- **Keys Conch:** a person born in the Florida Keys. You can be born in Miami and move to the Keys an hour later, then live down there the rest of your life, and you will still NEVER be a Conch. They are usually very tough and independent characters.
- **Lean Seat:** a high bench seat usually found behind the helm of a center console. Designed to be leaned against or sat upon. May have storage built-in under the seat section.
- **Mezzanine Deck:** a shallow, raised deck on a sportfish just forward of the fishing cockpit, and aft of the wheelhouse bulkhead. Usually contains aft-facing bench seating for anglers to comfortably watch the baits that are being trolled behind the boat.
- **Outriggers:** long aluminum poles on sportfishing boats that are raked up and aft from up alongside the wheelhouse. They are extended outward when fishing, having clips on lines that carry the fishing lines out away from the boat, creating a wider spread.
- **Pilot Boat:** a smaller boat designed to handle all kinds of seas, whose sole purpose is delivering and retrieving a

captain with extensive local knowledge to larger boats approaching or leaving a port.

- **Rod Holder:** As the name suggests, a device that a fishing rod butt is inserted into to hold it steady. There are recessed types that are mounted on covering boards, and exposed ones attached to railings or tower legs.
- **Salon:** a living room area of a boat's cabin.
- **Scuppers:** deck or cockpit drains.
- **SeaKeeper Gyro:** a stabilizing gyro that almost eliminates roll in boats.
- **Shaft:** attaches a propeller to the gear.
- **Sheer Line:** the rail edge where the foredeck meets the side of the hull.
- **Sonar/Fish Finder:** electronic underwater 'radar' that displays the sea floor, and anything between it and the boat.
- **Sportfisherman (Sportfish):** a unique style of boat designed specifically for fishing.
- **Spread:** the arrangement of the baits being towed while trolling.
- **Stem:** the forwardmost edge of the bow.
- **Stern:** the farthest aft part of the boat, also called the transom.
- **Tackle Center:** a cabinet in the fishing cockpit or the center console which holds hooks, swivels, leads, and other fishing supplies.
- **(Tuna) Tower:** an aluminum pipe structure located above the house or the flybridge designed to hold spotters or riders, and may or may not have an additional helm.
- **Transom:** stern.
- **Transom (Tuna) Door:** a door in the stern just above the waterline, designed for boating large fish, but also useful for retrieving swimmers and divers.
- **Trough:** the lowest point between waves.

- **Wheel (Propeller):** slang for a prop.
- **Wheel (Steering):** controls the boat's direction.
- **Wheelhouse (House):** the cabin section of a boat which sometimes contains an enclosed helm.

ABOUT THE AUTHOR

Don Rich is the author of the bestselling Coastal Adventure, Coastal Beginnings, and Mobjack Mysteries series. Don's books are set mainly in the mid-Atlantic because of his love for this stretch of coastline.

As a fifth-generation Florida native who grew up on the water, he has spent a good portion of his life on, in, under, or beside it. He now makes his home in central Virginia. When he's not writing or watching another fantastic mid-Atlantic sunset, he can often be found in a marina or boatyard somewhere around the Chesapeake Bay or the Atlantic, researching his next book.

Don loves to hear from readers, and you can reach him via email at contact@donrichbooks.com

ALSO BY DON RICH

Check my website www.DonRichBooks.com for a current list of all my book titles.

The Coastal Beginnings Series:

(The prelude to the Coastal Adventure Series)

- **COASTAL CHANGES**
- **COASTAL TREASURE**
- **COASTAL RULES**
- **COASTAL BLUFFS**

The Coastal Adventure Series:

- **COASTAL CONSPIRACY**
- **COASTAL COUSINS**
- **COASTAL PAYBACKS**
- **COASTAL TUNA**
- **COASTAL CATS**
- **COASTAL CAPER**
- **COASTAL CULPRIT**
- **COASTAL CURSE**
- **COASTAL JURY**
- **COASTAL CURRENCY**
- **COASTAL CRUISE**

The Mobjack Mysteries Series:

- **Mobjack Gamble** *(Coming in 2024)*

Other Books by Don Rich:

- **GhostWRITER**

Here's A Tropical Authors Novella by Deborah Brown, Nicholas Harvey, and Don Rich:

- **Priceless**

Go to my website at www.DonRichBooks.com for more information about joining my **Reader's Group**! And you can follow me on Facebook at: https://www.facebook.com/DonRichBooks

I'm also a member of TropicalAuthors.com, where you can find my latest books and those by dozens of my coastal writer friends!

www.ingramcontent.com/pod-product-compliance
Lightning Source LLC
Chambersburg PA
CBHW060420310726
48976CB00003B/1137